P9-CNC-351

SOUTH MEDIA CENTER
GRANDVILLE PUBLIC SCHOOLS

S

$17.25-97

Phantom
Victory

Phantom Victory

PAMELA F. SERVICE

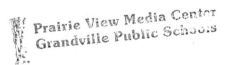
Prairie View Media Center
Grandville Public Schools

Atheneum Books for Young Readers

Atheneum Books for Young Readers
An imprint of Simon & Schuster Children's Publishing Division
1230 Avenue of the Americas
New York, New York 10020

Copyright © 1994 by Pamela F. Service
All rights reserved including the right of reproduction
in whole or in part in any form.

10   9   8   7   6   5   4   3

Printed in the United States of America

Library of Congress Cataloging-in-Publication Data
Service, Pamela F.
Phantom Victory / by Pamela F. Service—1st ed.
p.   cm.
Summary: A teenage boy and girl, aided by ancestral ghosts, embark
on a treasure hunt to find an heirloom necklace hidden years earlier
by a guest at South Bass Island's historic Victory Hotel.
ISBN 0-684-19441-4
[1. Hotels, motels, etc.— Fiction.
2. Islands—Fiction.
3. Ghosts—Fiction.   4. Mystery and detective stories.]   I. Title.
PZ7.S4885Ph   1994   [Fic]—dc20   93-37904

Most of my books are somewhat for Bob and Alex.
This one is especially.

Phantom Victory

1

Like some prehistoric monster, the fire reared up against the night sky. Its glowing body flared and twisted, while with ravenous roars it devoured its prey.

He stood among the other gawking islanders, among his fellow volunteer firemen, watching helplessly. Their Victory! Their huge, famous, elegant hotel, the focus of so many dreams and jobs and memories. Second by second it was vanishing in the flames.

As he watched he felt his life vanishing as well. A life already dimmed by *her* death eleven years ago, its only remaining spark had been the hotel. And soon it, too, would be nothing but smoke and ashes.

But they mustn't let that happen! Half the island had flocked here with buckets and willing arms. Surely something could be saved!

The fire hadn't really reached the front section yet. Silhouetted against the furnace glow, the main tower with its fantastic turrets remained untouched.

"Come on!" he yelled, charging forward. "We can still save something!"

The rising roar of flames drowned the voices of his comrades calling him back. Hopeful now, he ran across the lawn and up the main stairs. Inside, the grand lobby opened before him.

He stopped to catch his breath. Here the sound and heat of the inferno seemed held back. In the flickering, ruby light, everything seemed as he remembered it—not threadbare and run-down as it had become in recent years, but luxurious, with thick carpet and elegant furniture. Chandeliers tinkled, and he could hear an echo of the grand piano. Could some guest still be inside?

Alarmed, he looked around. There *was* someone. She stood in a lacy white dress at the top of the grand staircase. Her smile was calm and playful—not relief at seeing a rescuer, but pleasure at seeing *him.*

And he knew that smile. It reached his heart and filled the emptiness of eleven years. He had always known this. He'd always known they'd been wrong. She could never have drowned that day. He'd been waiting for her all these years, and now she'd come back. Come back to him and to their treasure. Blond head tilted, she waved in her impish, butterfly way, then sped down the oaken stairway toward him. With a cry of happiness he ran to meet her.

Ears filled with distant music and welcoming laughter, he never heard the warning shouts. He never heard the crack and boom as the flaming walls gave way and toppled down on him. He never heard his own scream.

But Terri heard it. It echoed in her scream. She had muffled that in the blankets bunched up around her face. Sitting hunched in bed she blinked at the placid morning light and shivered slightly in the cool July air. That air held no hint of acrid smoke or inferno heat. It never did.

Lying back, she tried to calm her lurching heart. The dream again—the fire dream. She hadn't had it in months, but it was always the same. It had been for years.

She sighed, disgusted with herself. Why did her mind keep doing this to her? You'd think it would get tired of playing the same tape over and over again. She knew what must have started it originally. When she was little her dad and others would talk about the famous Victory Hotel fire and how Great-uncle Joseph Graff had died trying to fight the blaze. But where that blond girl had come from Terri hadn't a clue. And the dream was always the same: always from inside Joe's mind, always the same longing memories, the same impossible vision.

And this same stupid dream always put her in a foul mood for the whole day. She snorted and sat up. If the day wasn't going to get worse, she'd better get up and not be late for work.

Rummaging in her drawers, she selected jeans and a T-shirt showing Garfield the cat expressing his general displeasure with the world. As far as wardrobe goes, she thought, she was lucky to have landed this particular summer job. Island kids almost always got summer jobs, but most were in shops or in other ways tied to the tourist trade, so they had to primp and look their best. But this year she was expected to root around in the dirt and so could dress accordingly.

It was a good job in other ways, too. The pay was great, and it was a lot more interesting than selling souvenirs or renting golf carts and bicycles to people who had no business being on either. When it had been announced that workers were being recruited to help excavate the old hotel site and maybe restore it, Terri's father had urged her to apply since her family had helped run the Victory in its heyday. And she had to admit, she'd always been fascinated with the old ruins and thought it sad that such a romantic, glamorous place should have burned to the ground.

Not that there was anything romantic or glamorous about scrabbling in the dirt and recording the broken pottery, melted glass, and twisted bedsprings she found. But if the scheme of rebuilding part of the place ever did work out, it would be terribly exciting.

Terri quickly ran a brush through her curly black hair and hurried downstairs. Her parents would already be at the shop, getting ready to sell postcards and fudge to today's batch of tourists. She poured cereal into a bowl, sloshed in some milk, and carried it out to the sun room, which had once been a pillared porch but was now walled in with big picture windows.

Curling up on a couch, Terri munched her cereal and looked absently at the familiar view. Through the leafy branches of an oak, the blue water of Lake Erie sparkled in the clear morning sunlight. The mainland of Ohio made a purple-green smudge along the horizon, and between it and their island, the water was already dotted with the white sails of pleasure boats. It was a perfect July day. She shuddered slightly. This meant that soon little South Bass Island would be overrun with day-tripping tourists. Already she could see the white spume of one of the car ferries plowing its way toward them from Catawba Point. And beyond that she could see the glint of one of the passenger ferries out of Port Clinton taking the longer loop around the island to disgorge its jabbering tourists on the village of Put-in-Bay.

For a moment something hazy came between her and the view. She blinked, then shrugged and went back to her cereal. It was only the Watching Boy. She'd seen him around the house as long as she could remember. Always watching out some window or other, sometimes, like now, standing half in, half out of some wall that hadn't always been there.

Her mother never saw him, but once her father had admitted that he used to. He'd also advised that it was best not to tell anyone about it. She had learned what he meant once when she'd told her class during show-and-tell that her house was haunted. They kidded her about it for years. Now she just accepted it. Some houses had mice, some had ghosts. And of the two, ghosts that just watched out windows were the least harmful.

Then she almost dropped her cereal. For the first time ever, the cloudy figure turned around. Instead of watching the expanse of lake and the spume of the ferryboats, the boy turned and looked at her.

His black hair was parted in the middle, and his large

dark eyes looked right into hers. He opened his mouth and said something, but Terri heard nothing except the swish of waves against the rocks below the house.

Terri thought that if he moved one step toward her, she would scream. But he didn't. He just gradually faded from sight.

Shakily, Terri stood up and walked to the kitchen. She stood at the sink, mechanically washing her cereal bowl and trying to think about routine, boring stuff. But her mind felt shattered. No, this was not starting out to be a good day.

2

Bucking and rolling, the ferry plunged steadily forward. Its blunt prow smacked down hard, kicking up a sheet of water that doused the kids who were running and laughing on the car deck below. Brian tried to ignore them. They and the other passengers seemed determined to enjoy this trip. He was determined not to.

The breeze scudded over the broad blue surface of Lake Erie, scattering it with whitecaps. It buffeted Brian's windbreaker and raked his shaggy blond hair across his eyes. Through it, squinting against the glare of sun on water, he watched the approaching island, the gray-green smudge slowly drawing nearer.

South Bass Island, he thought gloomily. Named after a fish, for crying out loud. How dull can you get? Of course, it sounded great to someone like Brian's dad, who wanted to spend two solid weeks fishing. But Brian knew, after many other such "vacations," that he hated fishing. It was so boring, staring hour after hour at a line in the water. And what's worse, he might catch something. Then he'd have to watch some poor fish flop about, drowning in the air because he, Brian Cornwell, had tricked it into driving a hook into its lip. Then he'd have to gut and eat the nasty thing. The only fish he could stand the taste of was canned tuna—with lots of pickles and mayonnaise.

It wasn't so bad when his dad dragged them somewhere halfway interesting on these trips—Florida or the Colorado Rockies, say. But this dumb island was still in Ohio, for crying out loud!

Of course, Brian knew there were special reasons for this choice—picking up some long-dead family tradition. As his dad told it, around the turn of the century the Cornwell family had been rolling in wealth, and they used to spend every summer at some expensive and fashionable resort hotel on South Bass Island. The fishing had been superb. Brian's grandfather had been a very little boy then, but years later he'd told his own son about the huge towered building like a fairy castle and the sloping green lawns he used to run down. But then his older sister had been drowned, and the family stopped coming to the island.

Apparently no Cornwell had been back since, but Brian's dad didn't see why dusty family sorrows should stand in the way of great fishing, particularly when it was so close to home. And the more reading Mr. Cornwell had done prior to this vacation, the more enthusiastic he had become about revisiting the family's old haunts and renewing the tie to their elegant past.

The idea didn't do a thing for Brian. The past, he figured, was past.

He continued gazing at the island, but it wasn't looking much better. In fact there was something about it that felt off. Maybe that was because as an island it was a flop. If you were going to be stuck on an island, it ought to at least have palm trees. There did seem to be plenty of trees, but they all looked like the ones back home, and the cliffs along the shoreline weren't all that dramatic. That old hotel had apparently burned some years after his family had stopped coming, so there wouldn't even be that to explore.

Below, some kids were throwing bread out to a screaming welcoming committee of sea gulls that wheeled and dove at the crumbs like bombers. Beyond them, Brian could now pick out buildings on the shore. Most obvious were a lighthouse at one end and, two-thirds of the way down the island, a tall slender column rising up as a monument to some battle or other. He'd read about it in a tourist brochure. He guessed that the tourist-trap town he'd also read about must be on the other side of the island—the sort of place that ought to draw his mother like honey. Quaint shops and a beach to lie on were all his mother demanded of a vacation.

Moodily Brian stared down into the water that churned beside their boat. The Great Cornwell Family Pilgrimage back to its roots. He wondered whether the island had been any fun when Grandfather and his sister had been kids here. Probably not. He bet Great-aunt Sophie hadn't drowned in a ferry accident, after all. She'd probably thrown herself off a cliff out of pure boredom. Good thing he'd brought a lot of books.

The morning had been bad enough already, and now she *was* going to be late for work. Before Terri had even rolled her bike out of the shed, she'd heard the blat of the ferry as it came in to dock. In her mind she could see the wide ramp clanging down and the foot passengers pouring out like eager sheep. They'd be followed by the noisy, smelly tide of cars and vans determined to clog the island's narrow roads despite pleas to leave cars on the mainland.

Now as she pedaled out of their private drive onto the main road, Terri found that the wave of cars was just going by. If she didn't hurry, she'd be caught up in the second and worse wave, the rented bicycles and golf carts.

By the time she reached the state park, Terri was hot and in an even worse mood. As she pulled up to the entrance, she glanced at a car packed with fishing and camping gear. A man was standing outside arguing with a park employee. Inside the car, a woman was almost hidden behind dark glasses and a floppy hat while a blond boy sprawled in the backseat looking thoroughly bored and miserable. Perversely the sight cheered Terri.

Go ahead, she thought, have a miserable time here. I didn't invite you. I've got better ways to spend my time than trashing someone else's island. I'm spending my summer doing something worthwhile.

Smugly she sped through the gate, then curved right along the road marked AUTHORIZED PERSONNEL ONLY. Hopping off, she walked her bike up the last stretch to the flat-topped hill.

The others, mostly high school kids like herself, were already at work in the marked-off squares, troweling, brushing, and sifting the dirt. Others at tables were cleaning and photographing the artifacts and placing them into marked bags.

Terri walked quickly to the office trailer to sign in, but just then Mr. Stephenson stepped out, his handsome, chiseled face clouding in a frown.

"Here's another late one," he said over his shoulder. "I tell you, Stew, we need to hire off-island professionals, not these native kids. They've got no sense of responsibility."

Keeping her blushing face lowered, Terri signed in and fumbled in a box for her supplies.

Stewart Kelso had stepped out after his partner. "Ease up, Keith. This is summer, remember. And, after all, if we actually pinpoint the hotel layout and raise enough money to secure a restoration grant, it will be these 'natives' who will benefit. We're just in it for fun, remember?"

The other man snorted. "Yeah, but if we do it right, there also ought to be a little return on our investment, you know."

Kelso laughed, running a plump hand through his thinning gray hair. "Right. Guess that business sense is why you're a self-made millionaire and I just inherited mine."

11

 Prairie View Media Center
Grandville Public Schools

Quietly Terri slipped off to her square of the excavation. Dr. Kelso, she liked. As a kid, he'd been one of the island's summer people, returning again and again to the same vacation home. She didn't mind that sort. She had regular returning friends among summer people. They cared about the island, not like the day-trippers who came to gawk and shop and party. Dr. Kelso had loved the island so much, he'd thought up this wild scheme to restore the Victory Hotel to its former glory—if he was able to raise enough money from developers like this Stephenson guy and through grants.

She did shudder a little at the idea of all the new tourists such a thing would bring, but it would also mean a lot of good-paying jobs for the locals, and maybe as much fame and prosperity for the island as when the Victory was here the first time.

As she brushed away dirt from a tangle of twisted metal and glass, Terri thought about all the pictures she'd seen of the place. The fantastic turreted building, the sweeping lawns with their scenic walks and romantic grottoes. The busy trolley cars and all the beautiful people strolling on the verandas or enjoying outdoor concerts. It was exciting to think of actually helping to bring all of that back.

She guessed her father was right: The Graff family and the hotel were meant to be linked. After all, her great-grandfather had been a hotel superintendent, and nearly everyone in the family had had some job at the place—cutting grass or doing laundry or maybe serving the elegant meals. And Great-uncle Joe had died trying to put out the fire.

The thought made her shiver as if the sun had passed behind a cloud—a cloud of smoke. She saw again the glowing red towers, the sweeping staircase, heard the crackling flames and the chandeliers tinkling in the rising heat. Blankly she looked down at the melted lump of glass in her hand, then dropped it as if it were hot. It might have been part of that chandelier.

"Idiot," she whispered, trying to force her mind back to the present. But the sudden feeling of cold would not leave. It was the cold of fear; fear of the past. She shook her head. No, it was not the past itself she feared, but what it was doing to her. It was creeping into her life. The phantom in her house, the horrid recurring dream. She wished desperately that they would leave her alone.

3

Brian scrunched down in the backseat, trying to ignore the rest of the world. Outside the car his father was arguing with some park person. Listlessly he glanced out the window to see a dark-haired girl skim arrogantly by on her bicycle. He closed his eyes, trying to look cool or asleep.

Then the car was underway again while his father ranted that more than half the campground was closed because some archaeologists were digging around in the remains of the old hotel. All the remaining campsites were taken, but the ranger had said they could cruise around until they saw someone packing, about to free up a site.

At least this was something to do. Brian gazed like a vulture out the window as they circled through the campground until they swooped down on a site where a young couple was just packing up their tent. Then, for a while, the mechanics of setting up camp took his attention. After some debate they placed his parents' tent on a flat spot near the campfire ring, and he sited his own on a tree-enclosed bluff overlooking the lake. His mother fussed over his choice, but she finally gave in with an admonition not to take up sleep-walking.

Brian declined to join his parents when they went off to see about the fishing boat they'd arranged to rent. He also rejected the idea of renting a golf cart or a bike for himself. This island was so puny that if he had a vehicle he'd see the whole place in a day and a half and have nothing to do for the rest of the two weeks. To survive he'd have to sandwich exploring on foot between lots of reading.

He'd begin explorations, he decided, with the beach below their campsite. After searching for the easiest route, he followed a weedy gully that cut through the cliff to the water's edge. This was no tourist-brochure beach with a broad stretch of soft white sand. The rocky cliffs walled in a narrow crescent of gray, water-worn pebbles that shifted and clattered under his feet at every step. With a steady slap and hiss, the waves darkened the lowest fringe of rocks with shining dampness.

Brian reached down and picked up a flat stone and a piece of green glass smoothed and frosted by the waves. He dropped the glass into his pocket. Then, flicking his wrist, he skipped the stone in a lazy double arch over the ruffled water. Two weeks with rock skipping as a major pastime should improve his technique.

Walking along over the noisily shifting stones, he came to several large broken slabs of concrete. The lower ones, slanting down into the water, were covered with slimy green moss that swayed back and forth in the waves like long green hair—the hair of someone who had drowned.

Like that great-aunt of his, maybe. Despite the warmth of the sun, he shivered. Of course, his great-aunt Sophie had never looked like a great-aunt. She'd died when she was young—his age maybe. He looked down again. This concrete had probably been part of some dock or walkway at the hotel. She could have stood right here, watching the crinkly blue water and dreaming of getting away from here. Brian tried to shake off the creepiness of the thought. It was just a piece of broken concrete, for crying out loud.

Reaching down for another flat stone, he launched it into a triple skip. But Sophie slid back into his thoughts. Maybe she hadn't wanted to escape from here. Maybe this island was something to escape *to*. After all, from what he'd read, Victorian girls weren't given much chance for freedom and adventure. Maybe summers at an island resort seemed a lot better than tea parties in parlors and going to a girls' "finishing school." Maybe . . .

Oh, who cares? Angrily he grabbed up a handful of pebbles and hurled them all in. Why was he cluttering his mind with Sophie Cornwell? She was dead and gone, and so were her opinions. They didn't matter now, any more than what he cared about would matter to people a century from now—he snorted angrily. Or to a lot of people right now, it seemed.

He climbed back up to the campsite, taking some comfort from the sight of all the books he'd stacked in his tent. But the little yellow cocoon was too hot and airless for comfortable reading, so he grabbed a half-finished paperback and set out for the upper portion of the campground in search of a secluded reading spot.

He followed the looping road up a wooded hill. In one tree a squirrel and a blue jay were carrying on a heated argument, but otherwise the campground was heavy with midday silence. Before long, his road was cut off by a shiny new cyclone fence. Resentfully he stared through the metal mesh.

That was certainly the prime part of the campground, but he didn't see any old ruins. He didn't see any archaeological-looking people either. He bet this whole thing was just a parks-service trick to keep down the number of people staying here.

Well, *he* was staying here, and he wasn't in the mood to let any Smoky Bear types tell him where he could and couldn't go. A few feet to his right the fence spanned a small gully, leaving a wedge-shaped crawl space below.

In seconds he was standing triumphantly on the other side, brushing the dirt from his jeans. Suddenly everything on this forbidden side of the fence looked far more interesting than on the other. There must be something here worth seeing, or they wouldn't have fenced it off.

He began strolling over the flat hilltop, eyes on the ground. The place was certainly strewn with stuff that wasn't your average campground litter. There were bricks, shards of broken pottery, and countless glints of broken glass.

Squatting down, he pulled an old square nail out of the dirt and used it to scrape around. There were fragments of shiny brown china and some that were white with blue flowers. And here was a piece of flat glass with a funny metal grid pattern on one side. Must have been part of a window, and the window screen melted right into the glass. Cool.

Dropping these treasures into a pocket, he continued and pulled free a bottle all twisted and folded over on itself. That must have been quite some fire, he thought. This could have been a syrup bottle or a—

"And what do you think you're doing here?"

Brian nearly dropped the melted bottle. "Oh, just poking around."

The person standing over him was a girl with curly black hair and angry eyes. "Well, you can go poke somewhere else. This is the Victory Hotel site, and only proper excavation is allowed."

"I don't see any excavating going on."

"You also don't see signs or fences, it seems."

Brian stood up so that he was eye to eye with the girl. "Hey, we paid to stay in this campground, and there's no reason for you dirt grubbers to hog so much of it."

The girl tossed her hair out of her eyes. "There happens to be plenty of reason. If we find enough evidence here and raise enough money, we're going to rebuild the Victory Hotel. Then we'll have a lot better class of visitors than your sort staying here again."

She snatched the melted bottle out of his hand. "But if amateurs like you keep messing around, you'll ruin everything."

"Amateurs! Oh, I suppose you're a big-time professional archaeologist. The Indiana Jones of South Bass Island."

"I'm learning. Besides," she said, defiantly sticking the old bottle back into the dirt, "I'm a Graff. Terri Graff. Graffs have always worked at this hotel. My great-grandfather was a superintendent here. I even had a great-uncle who died trying to put out the fire."

"So I'm supposed to fall down and worship? Well, if you're going to flaunt dead ancestors, my great-grandparents used to *stay* in this hotel. They were the ones ordering your dead ancestors around."

Triumphantly Brian turned on his heel and tromped back down the hill. So, family history does have its uses, he thought smugly. But slowly his elation faded. An odd feeling was creeping over him, almost as if he were being watched. Despite himself he glanced around, but the campground seemed deserted. Still, he half wished that he and that girl hadn't said what they had just now. Somehow this didn't seem the place or the time to evoke dead ancestors.

Walking through the deathly silence of the woods, he

19

felt very uneasy. This island wasn't just boring and un-friendly, it was creepy. There was something here, and there had been, he realized, since he'd first seen the is-land. Something that was circling him, buzzing around like some bloodthirsty insect. It was nothing he could swat at or hide from. And he did not like it.

This was going to be a very long two weeks.

4

The moon was so bright it appeared as a glowing smudge on his tent roof, as if it would coldly burn its way through the thin nylon skin and shine directly on him. The insects were just as intense. From high up in the canopy of trees, they sang their steady summer chants. Sort of like a cross between lawn sprinklers and smoke detectors, Brian thought, but he couldn't decide whether they were soothing or annoying. They were certainly loud.

He rolled over, hot and sticky even though his sleeping bag was unzipped. It always took a few nights to get used to the discomfort and odd noises of camping. But tonight Brian knew it was more than just those things keeping him awake.

He hadn't been able to shake the creepy feeling that had come on him this afternoon. It was like coming down with the flu or something, only the oddness was spreading from outside of him. The Cornwells had been right to stop coming back to this island. Even now, it might be better if they were staying in some bed-

and-breakfast place instead of camping on the site of their family's old resort. It sounded crazy and he wanted to deny it—but he couldn't. There was something here that seemed to be reaching out for him, something familiar yet frighteningly strange. Something that seemed to have been waiting for him.

Boy, you're weird, Brian, he said to himself. You ought to write scripts for horror movies or something. So the place is a little creepy. Only a superstitious, melodramatic nerd would try to keep from being bored to death by scaring himself to death instead.

He sat up. There was no point in lying here freaking himself out. Unzipping the tent doorway, he sat half in and half out of the little arched opening, looking out at the moonlit world. The dark lake glittered with wave-shattered moonlight. Across it cut the engine roar and cheery lights of a ferryboat, probably taking the night's last batch of revelers back to the mainland.

On the lake's far shore, silhouetted against the sky glow of a distant city, rose the distinctive dark tower of a nuclear power plant. Like baleful eyes, red lights blinked from its top to warn away aircraft. Now, there was something solid and real to feel creepy about. No need to make up vague thoughts of family curses.

Brian stood up and looked around. A pretty ordinary campground, really. The two college guys in the next campsite had finally turned off their boom box, and all was silent and asleep except for the insects sawing away in the tops of their trees.

No, there was someone else awake. Someone in a white nightgown, probably setting off on a trek to the latrine. Idly he watched the pale figure move through the trees. It wasn't heading along the route he'd expect, but cutting up the slope, near where he'd gone today. As it disappeared over the top of the hill, he realized suddenly that it must be way beyond the fence, though he hadn't noticed the person stoop or scramble over anything. There must actually be a gate up there.

But why would a camper head up that way? He laughed as the answer hit him. There'd be lots of unused latrines up there, ones a lot nicer-smelling and freer of flies than the ones down here. So this camper in the white nightgown had her own private latrine. Score one for campers versus snooty archaeologists.

Sitting down on the cold ground, Brian turned his attention back to the lake. The departing ferry was now just a receding dot of light. He watched it as it moved among the fixed lights of the far shore until his eyes ached and he felt sleepy enough to crawl back into his sleeping bag. But first, a visit to the latrine wouldn't be a bad idea.

He stood up and stretched. Why not try that girl's secret spot? She was no doubt already tucked back into her tent. Wow, an exciting moonlight adventure. The quest for the unsmelly latrine!

Pulling on shoes and a jacket, he headed up the slope. The fence could be seen between the bushy shadows, a silver mesh catching the moonlight like a giant spiderweb.

The girl had crossed between those two huge oaks, yet he couldn't find any kind of gate. He walked farther along the fence but saw no break at all.

Slowing to a stop, he ran a puzzled hand through his pale tousled hair. Not that it mattered, really. His father thought it was macho not to complain about smelly latrines, and he certainly wasn't going to spend the night searching the hills for a mythical new one. But still it was a mystery, and petty or not, he hated unsolved mysteries.

He was just turning away when he noticed something on the other side of the fence, something white and flapping. For an embarrassed second, he thought it was the girl coming back, but then he realized it was something lying on a rock, ruffling in the faint night breeze. It looked like an open book or notebook—something belonging to one of the archaeologists, maybe.

The thought kindled a spark of interest. There might be something worth seeing in it—pictures of the way the old hotel used to look, or even sketches of what had been dug up. He wouldn't admit to the park people that he cared a fig about it, not after his run-in with that snooty girl, but just the same he *was* kind of interested. And why shouldn't he be? After all, the Cornwells must once have spent a fortune here, staying in the posh place.

With defiant delight he traced the fence to where the gully cut under it and soon was on the other side, pushing his way through the scrub to the notebook lying on the rock. He reached toward it, then guiltily jumped back. Had something moved among the trees? No— only moonlight and shadows.

Sitting on the moss-splotched stone, Brian picked up the book and began leafing through it. No pictures or

24

diagrams. Just pages and pages of handwriting with dates at the tops. The light wasn't good enough to read much. The whole thing looked rather old, faded, and boring.

Annoyed, he closed the book, plunking it back onto the rock. In the moonlight the cover looked a pale pink, and he could see that someone had decorated it with little ink drawings of flowers and birds. In fancy handwriting several words nestled among the pictures, words large enough to read even in this light.

A sudden chill blew through him. All his earlier uneasiness tightened into a hard, cold knot. Like a frightened animal, he wanted to run, but all he could do was sit there and stare. *Diary,* the fancy lettering said. *Diary of Sophie Anne Cornwell, 1908.*

5

For long moments Brian just sat there, his mind furiously arguing with itself. That book had been lying there, waiting for him. He didn't want anything to do with it, or with whatever had led him to it. He didn't want anything to do with this whole creepy island.

But in a way, that diary was his. *Cornwell,* his name, was written right on it. It had been written by his own great-aunt, his grandfather's sister.

Besides, what was really so freaky about this? Like his mom said, he just watched too many creepy movies. It was perfectly logical for these archaeologists to be using diaries written by people who'd once stayed at the hotel. They'd probably describe things and save the diggers a lot of trouble. It was just coincidence, for crying out loud, and he ought to take advantage of it.

Hesitantly he reached out and touched the book again. No earth tremor, no flash of lightning. Picking it up, he slipped the diary into his jacket pocket. He'd read the thing and then maybe return it to the park people or the archaeologists—someone other than that girl.

Refusing to let his thoughts stray into any creepier territory, he headed back to the fence and the camp-ground.

Terri swatted at a fly that was buzzing annoyingly around her tray of newly washed potsherds. Today was worse than yesterday, she decided as she continued slushing muddy bits of pottery through the washtubs on one of the dig tables. No recurring dreams or super-natural appearances—just bothersome living people.

Actually it was largely one person, but he was enough. Shortly after she and the others had arrived for work, Keith Stephenson had apparently discovered something missing—some old diary he'd been using for research. He began barging around the dig camp, then tearing through his and Dr. Kelso's trailers look-ing for it.

Next he'd turned on the excavation workers them-selves, frantically searching through their things and all but accusing each one of stealing the diary. Here Kelso had tried to intervene, but Stephenson wouldn't be put off, and one of the workers had quit in a huff, saying she wouldn't work for someone who accused her of theft.

Terri had been tempted to do the same, except that each day she felt more and more committed to the pro-ject. She wanted to help make it succeed and wasn't going to let one adult nut case put her off.

Besides, she felt kind of protective toward Dr. Kelso. He'd been a friend of the island for so long, and was such a mild-mannered guy, it just didn't seem right to walk off and leave him in the hands of a maniac like Stephenson. A lot of money for the dig might be coming from Stephenson, but the idea and the real commitment were Kelso's.

And right now he was still trying to calm his partner down. "Okay, Keith," he was saying, not far from Terri's table. "Let's go over this again. You were using it yesterday, right?"

"Yes, yes," Stephenson answered, distractedly raking a hand through his graying blond hair. "But it was too noisy here with all those supposed workers jabbering away."

Terri felt a flush of indignation but lowered her head and kept eavesdropping.

"So then you went off with it somewhere."

"Right," Stephenson continued, "we've gone over all this before. I packed it, a notebook, and some old guidebooks into a tote bag and trekked off somewhere quiet to try to piece things together. I spread them all out on a big flat rock over by the fence. When I finished I thought I packed everything back in the bag, but now the diary's missing. It simply must have been stolen."

Dr. Kelso shook his head. "Not likely. It wouldn't have much value to anyone but us. Besides, it isn't as though we've lost the information, since we do have your photo copies. In fact I'm surprised you were using the original. After all, you haven't let me even open the cover."

"I know, I know. I guess I feel pretty possessive about it. If I hadn't found the thing in that Sandusky antique shop, I never would have gotten interested in financing this project. But it's just the sort of thing some kid might try to sell to an antique dealer for a few bucks."

Kelso only snorted.

"Okay," Stephenson went on, "how about someone thinking it contained useful information? Half the people on this backward island seem to think we're digging for buried treasure. I bet that's why a lot of this precious crew you hired signed on. I wouldn't put it past any of them to lift the thing."

As Kelso mildly argued back, Terri didn't bother to feel indignant. Her thoughts were swirling around Stephenson's description of where he'd been reading the diary—a flat rock near the fence. That was near where she'd found that jerk poking about yesterday. Could he have found the diary? He was just the sort of ignorant clod who might think he could sell it or use it to find buried treasure. She started getting mad at him all over again.

She wouldn't mention anything to Stephenson yet in case he nastily accused her of just trying to cover up her own theft. It was probably a false trail anyway, but she'd check it out after work.

It was four o'clock when she left the dig that afternoon, but instead of biking home, she cruised slowly around the looping roads of the lower campground. Most of the campers were away: off fishing, or lying on the beach giving themselves skin cancer, or spending money in town. But several were puttering around their camps, and one blond boy was reading alone at a picnic table.

She couldn't believe her luck. It was the same jerk tourist. But suddenly she didn't feel like marching right up and accusing him of theft. She'd try to be more subtle.

Parking her bike she sauntered over to the campsite, but the boy didn't notice, he was so engrossed in his reading. Be like a TV detective, she told herself, stepping closer. Just making a few routine inquiries, sir. Just—

Suddenly her whole insides clenched. That kid was reading something yellowed and handwritten. It looked a lot like an old diary.

"Excuse me," she said bluntly. "What are you reading?"

The boy jerked and looked up. His eyes widened, then he flushed as if a bucket of red paint had been thrown over his face. "I . . . It's just something I found."

She tried for a menacing squint. "A dairy, maybe?"

Abruptly he slapped the book closed, spreading his hands over the cover. "Yeah, a diary; an old family diary. Any law against reading diaries?"

"No," she said, trying to get a peep at the cover through his spread fingers, "just against stealing them."

His face turned as pale as it had been red before. "So, who's stolen anything? This is my great-aunt Sophie's diary. See?" He cautiously lifted his hands. "Sophie Anne Cornwell. That's my name—Cornwell. Brian Cornwell. Want to see my ID or something?"

Terri felt confused, but had no intention of backing down. "Save that for the police."

Now the boy stood up, looking more angry than scared. "Hey, cut out the tough-cop act. I found this thing up by the fence. Someone had just left it on a rock. It could have gotten rained on or anything. I was going to turn it over to the park people, but I wanted to read it first. After all she *was* my great-aunt."

"So, have you read it?"

"Several times."

"Fine, then I'll take it back."

She reached for the book, but Brian snatched it up first. "Not so fast. Have you read it?"

"I've seen the photocopies."

"It's been copied?"

"Of course. Mr. Stephenson found it in an antique shop and has been using it to locate some of the things around here."

"I bet he has. So you've all read it?"

"Well, none of us diggers have. Dr. Kelso and Mr. Stephenson are running the show."

"And cutting you out of the deal."

"What? Look, they're paying us good summer wages, and on top of it, we might get a restored hotel. Now hand the thing over. I'll just tell them some camper found it and turned it in. No questions asked."

From his expression the boy seemed to be juggling several ideas. Then he quickly opened the dairy to the back, pulled out a yellowed envelope, and held on to it while handing Terri the diary.

"I meant hand it *all* over," she said, grabbing the book.

"I did. You've got the diary. I've got this. It's . . . a let-

31

ter from my great-aunt. I ought to be able to keep some memento of her, for crying out loud. If your bosses want it back, tell them it's family property we're talking about." He smiled kind of wickedly, Terri thought. "And if that bothers them, maybe we'll just have to turn it over to the historical society or someone to publish."

Terri started to protest, but she had the feeling this kid was playing some game where she didn't know all the rules. Well, at least she had what she'd come for. Tightly clutching the diary, she gave the boy a parting glower and stalked back to her bike.

She'd almost reached it when he called after her, "You might read it yourself before turning it in, or you'll never know what you could be missing."

Brian smiled as he watched the girl pedal down the road, surprised he wasn't more angry. But after all, he'd won this one. She never looked back, but rode off, ramrod straight, her curly black hair bouncing about her shoulders. Too bad she's such a jerk, he thought. She looked like just the sort of girl it would be great to brag to the guys back home that he'd met on his summer vacation. But he was never much good at meeting girls, summer or not. And he didn't even know her name. Oh well, he—

Suddenly his thoughts jolted to a halt, then jumped backward. He did know her name. She'd said it yesterday. No wonder that name in the diary had seemed itchingly familiar. A cold spot in his stomach began to spread.

Another coincidence? That was getting a little thin, and he was getting a little scared—and a little angry.

Something on this island was jerking him around, messing with his life. He didn't like it. And he liked even less thinking about what that something was.

Suddenly he wished that Terri Graff *would* read the diary. He'd only said that to try to stir up trouble in their excavation camp. Just like he'd kept the envelope, with the idea of having a fleeting crack at adventure.

But now? He had the feeling he was being sucked into some sort of weird whirlpool. And somehow he'd feel a bit better if he wasn't going down alone.

6

Terri slowed her pace. The worst of her anger was evaporating along with the sweat she'd worked up from her furious pedaling. What a jerk that kid was, and what had he been driving at anyway? Something she wasn't picking up on—something about the contents of this diary. She felt its square-cornered weight in her windbreaker pocket.

As she sailed by the island's familiar landscapes, she thought about the little book. She wouldn't mind reading it, actually, even if that Brian guy had been egging her on to do just that. She'd seen the copy once when Dr. Kelso was reading it, but it hadn't seemed this thick. It should be pretty interesting, though, a diary kept by a girl staying at the Victory. And she might as well read it, since she wouldn't be turning it in until morning.

When she got home she rummaged around in the kitchen for a snack, then started to carry the chips, Coke, and diary into the sun room. But remembering the odd behavior yesterday of their supernatural tenant, she decided against it. She didn't want anyone who wasn't really there reading over her shoulder.

Instead she headed for one of her favorite rocks on the little beach in front of their house. The breeze pleasantly ruffled the air as she nestled into the smooth, sun-warmed hollow in the stone. A few feet away, waves lapped steadily among the pebbles. She opened the diary and began to read.

The account began January 1, 1908. Terri thought she'd skip through the winter and spring months when Sophie was still at her family's home in Cleveland. The problem was that Sophie managed to make everything so interesting, Terri couldn't force herself to skim. She ended up reading all about Sophie's schoolmates, neighbors, and family. Sophie seemed to have lively opinions about all of them and about everything else that came into her life.

There were parties and visits, jokes and arguments, gifts she made, poems she wrote, pranks she played, and a number of harebrained schemes that Sophie and her friends launched into, and at which they usually avoided getting caught. Accounts of the time at the debutante ball when they slipped goldfish into the punch and the time they dressed as boys so that they could gallivant around the city at night, made hilarious stories. Terri was sure this diary had been kept well hidden from Sophie's parents. She realized, too, that if Sophie Cornwell were alive today, she would like her very much.

Then came the excited flurry when Sophie, her mother, father, and baby brother packed up for their yearly trip to South Bass Island and the Victory Hotel. Sophie was looking forward to it. She loved the beaches and the fairy-tale castle of a hotel and the friends she had among the regular guests. And then, of course, there was Joe Graff.

Graff. Joe Graff, Terri repeated to herself. Despite the warmth of the late-afternoon sun, a chill shivered through her. Sophie Cornwell had been a friend of Great-uncle Joe's, the hotel superintendent's oldest son, the young man who later died in the fire.

Slowly the sun dipped toward the smear of mainland to the west. Above the steady plash of waves, the sounds of Terri's parents returning from work floated down from the house on the bluff. But Terri was aware only of the faded words on the pages before her.

When the trolley car from Put-in-Bay finally stopped in front of the hotel, Sophie reported, "Somehow, we managed to get me, Papa, Mama, Baby Clarence, and Mrs. Twite, his new nurse, plus all the trunks and bags, off the trolley and disentangled from the other passengers. Then, in the midst of all the fuss, I looked at the front walk and there was Joe, that same calm smile on his face.

"You know, Diary, it felt awfully good seeing him there (not that I would ever tell him so). But I could not help thinking of the girls back home getting all simpery over some boy or other, like Lydia over that big oaf Ronald. Of course I can gossip and even flirt with the best of them, but I always know that Joe is waiting back here on this island—not some sappy 'boyfriend,' but a friend who is a boy. Someone who is always ready to scramble over the cliffs like a mountain goat, or just sit on the rocks and talk about life, or plan some prank on another hotel guest, or trade jokes and insults with me—giving every bit as good as he gets.

"That was such fun we had last summer, that spy game, pretending we were spies for the prince of Montenegro and hiding in the Serbian royal court. Passing coded messages back and forth, figuring out which of the other guests were spies for which country—sometimes following them all over the island, trying not to be noticed. Then there was the time we managed to upset the vegetable delivery cart because we were pretending it was the secret conveyance of an anarchist bomb thrower.

"This summer I am determined to think up something even better. Sometimes I think the only time I am truly alive is these summer months at the Victory. And I do want this to be a lively summer."

Terri continued reading, hardly noticing when the sun slipped around the western headland, spreading a cool purple shadow over the beach. Eventually her mother found her and dragged her back to the house for dinner, though nothing about the dinner-table conversation did much to drag Terri's mind back from 1908. When her father teased her about being off on a cloud somewhere, she was tempted to tell her parents all about the diary, but then decided to keep it special to herself a little longer.

After dinner she slipped up to her room, curled onto her bed amid a nest of pillows and stuffed animals, and continued reading.

37

"Mama gave me the most dreadful lecture," Sophie reported two days after their arrival at the Victory. "She took me into her room this morning and said in that firm velvety way of hers that this summer, now that I am all of fourteen, she expects me to start acting like a young lady. She does not wish me to go running all over the island like a wild pony, and she wants me to spend more time with the nice young people of quality who are *staying* at the hotel and less with locals who simply *work* here.

"Well, I started arguing that the job Joe's father had of helping to run this hotel was every bit as respectable as Papa's job of running banks, but she told me not to talk back, and then Clarence woke up and started bawling, so I was able to make my escape.

"I was so angry, though, that right after lunch (a good one with my favorite stuffed mangoes on the menu, as well as chicken mayonnaise) I sought out Joe, who was helping the dining room manager with the silver inventory, and he took me on a tour of all the new things that have been added to the grounds since last summer. The walkways have been extended for more fine views of Sunset Rocks, and they have put in a good deal of new landscaping around the Natatorium and the Victory statue. I remember how muddy it was around the statue last August when they held the dedication ceremonies in the pouring rain. Some of the little ones had a really grand time of it splashing in the puddles until they moved the ceremonies inside. But now there are flowers all around, and Victory looks quite lovely on her pedestal with her wings and that daringly clingy Greek dress."

Next day Sophie reported, "Dear Diary, I am saved— or at least temporarily reprieved. I overheard Papa and Mama discussing me (*arguing* might be the more accurate, though less genteel, word). He disagreed with Mama's decision that this was my summer to be a grown-up, boring young lady. He pointed out that my coming-out ball was nearly two years off and said that I really should be allowed one more summer of being a little girl.

"Well, you know, dearest Diary, how in favor I am of women having as much say as men in the household and even having the right to vote. When I am old enough I think I might join those suffragette marches, though that would absolutely scandalize my family. But for this once I am awfully glad that Mama felt she had to meekly give in to the wishes of her husband. So, for this summer, instead of gossiping on the veranda or listening to tedious concerts on the lawn, I can be skipping rocks on the beach or even exploring caves with Joe.

"But if this is really to be my last summer of freedom, then I must make it a phenomenally spectacular one. I really must think of something grand to liven it up."

Terri kept reading every word. She could see how the diary would be of use to archaeologists, since Sophie described things in such detail. But then she found the next installment, written three days later, in what was becoming even better than a TV miniseries.

"Cybil and I spent the morning in the Natatorium. Cybil says her mother does not quite approve of letting men and women swim together, but since it is being done first here at the Victory, she feels it will be setting fashion for all the other grand resorts. Cybil is a perfect goose about being in the forefront of fashion, but the Natatorium is fun.

"At lunch Mama scolded me for eating like a horse, but I was hungry after all that swimming. Afterward I was thinking of taking the trolley into Put-in-Bay with some of the other girls, but Mama took so long fussing with my new white frock that I missed the trolley. I ran into Joe as I was walking back, and he said I looked very nice in the frock, and then he spoiled it by adding that I looked so grown-up I clearly would have no time for him or climbing cliffs anymore.

"Well, that made me so furious I practically hauled him off to go scaling cliffs—the ones north of the lighthouse. It did not do my new frock any good, but I guess that serves it right.

"But, dearest Diary, the best part is that on this excursion we started making plans for this summer's Great Game. It will be more daring and dangerous than any of them. This will show Joe just who is too grown-up! If it works, no one but the two of us will ever know that it happened. Oh, I don't ever want to be 'too grown-up' for this sort of fun!"

Eagerly Terri read ahead, looking for another reference to the Great Game. "Today was the day I resolved to do it, the Big Dastardly Deed. Actually, it wasn't very difficult. I suppose it would have been a more worthy challenge if I had been compelled to scramble up a wall and through barred windows like a cat burglar. But still, I was as nervous as if I had done that. With Papa back on the mainland because of some bank things, all I had to do was wait until Mama was downstairs playing bridge with the ladies and Mrs. Twite was taking Clarence out for his stroll.

"Then I slipped into Mama's room, took the key from the hat-pin jar, unlocked the drawer where she keeps her jewelry, and opened the leather case way in the back. Really, Mama should keep this thing in the hotel safe. Suppose I had been a real, for-keeps burglar?

"But anyway, there it was, the emeralds and diamonds and delicate gold flowers of Catherine the Great's necklace. Not that I totally believe the family story about it once belonging to that old Russian empress, but it certainly is beautiful enough to have. And it surely is worth a fortune no matter whose neck it has been around.

"I had brought along the beaded bag Aunt Belle gave me, the black one that's so ugly, and slipped the necklace inside after wrapping it in a silk scarf. And then, although I wanted to run away like a fox with a snatched chicken, I put everything carefully back so that no one would guess a thing. Mama never wears the necklace until the End-of-Season Ball, so there will be plenty of time to hide it, work out the clues, and then see how long it takes Joe to track it down. He is always going on about how clever island people are compared to mainlanders. We will just see, will we not?"

41

Three days later. "Dear Diary, this game is so terribly exciting that I would like to share every moment with you, but I dare not. Suppose you, my most intimate journal, were to fall into the Wrong Hands? Therefore, when I am engaged in the secret parts of this game such as hiding the treasure (as I did today) or laying down the clues, I must not note down any details that might give too much away.

"Joe and I have agreed that I will write all the clues on a single sheet of paper and give it to him in some secret way next Monday. In the meantime, though, I will keep the sheet with you, tucked into your back pages, for the clues are too cryptic for a casual spy. But as always, I will take the best care of you, dearest Diary, so you need have no fear of falling into the hands of spying Serbians—even if that was last summer's game."

Terri sat back. It seemed ages ago that her mother had called that it was time for bed and to turn out the light. But now she was much too caught up in this old, forgotten game.

At a sudden thought she flipped through the back of the diary, but then shook her head. The clues wouldn't be there. Sophie had turned them over to Joe years ago, and the game had been played out. Still, she wished Sophie had committed a little more to the diary. Having followed along this far only to be left out now was sort of like being told by good friends that she couldn't play with them anymore.

Terri yawned hugely, but she couldn't give up now. Flipping through the following pages, she hoped to find more snippets about the game. But Sophie was being very coy, talking about everything else.

Then Terri turned a page, and the words leaped at her. "Disaster! Oh, dear Diary, what am I to do? Not only is the game ruined, but so am I—and Joe, too, if I cannot manage to fix things, and I do not know how! I feel like throwing open my window and screaming 'Help!' loud and long."

Terri had been almost nodding asleep, but reading this jolted her awake. It was almost as if she could hear that cry. Instinctively she glanced up at her own open window, then back to her book.

Her face froze. Slowly she looked up again. Yes, she had seen him. The Watching Boy. Transparent as glass, but there, standing by her window. She had never seen him in her room before. Always he had been down-stairs, watching out some window for something as phantasmal as himself.

But now he was up here—and not watching out the window. He was watching her.

7

Gasping, Terri scooched down under the covers, pulling them over her head. The only sound was the frightened hammering of her heart.

Of course it was a nothing out there—nothing real. Only a phantom or figment or something. But just the same, she didn't want to look at it looking at her. Still she had to keep reading. That thing had popped in at the worst possible moment. She had to know what Sophie's awful disaster was.

Cautiously she stuck a hand from under the covers, switched off the bedside light, and fumbled around for the cold cylinder of her flashlight. She cringed at the thought of something filmy brushing against her wrist, but nothing did. Puffing the covers up into a stuffy little cave, she flicked on the flashlight and defiantly continued to read.

"Let me try to explain this to you calmly. Today was ordinary enough until after dinner. Of course, there have been rumors flying around all summer about how the Victory Hotel is in financial trouble. Papa and

44

Mama have talked about it lots and have even whispered that if Mr. McCreary, the manager, could not manage to improve things financially, the hotel might have to close.

"That is a dreadful thought, and it has made me nearly sick every time someone has mentioned it. I cannot imagine life without the Victory. I have not even mentioned it to you, dear Diary, because there was no point in making you unhappy, too. But now it cannot be helped.

"After supper Mama left our table and joined Mr. McCreary at his. He tapped on his glass until everyone in the room was quiet, and Mama began to speak in her most impressive foghorn voice. She said that everyone had undoubtedly heard rumors about how this dear hotel was having financial difficulties, ones that even threatened to prevent it from serving its loyal patrons in the future.

"Doubtless they all felt as distressed over this as did she, she continued, once the murmuring had quieted. The Victory was an important part of her and her family's lives. But quite suddenly she had realized that she need not stand helplessly by and watch this happen. She could and would do something about it.

"Then she went on to say that perhaps they would remember the heirloom necklace that she wears each year at the End-of-Season Ball. Well, she had decided to pledge that necklace to Mr. McCreary so that he might use it to help save the Victory. Those diamonds and emeralds were indeed precious, but the Victory Hotel and the years of happiness it represented were more precious still. If others there felt the same, she urged them to make similar gestures.

"The applause was thunderous, and Papa was beaming with pride. I should have been, too. My parents were helping to save my beloved hotel. Instead I felt about as sick as a person can without making a mess. Worse was to follow.

"Mr. McCreary stood up and made an eloquent speech of appreciation and announced that Mrs. Cornwell was planning to break her tradition and wear the necklace at the Midseason Ball this Saturday. At midnight she would turn it over to him on behalf of the Victory Hotel. Then he waved around a paper that she and Papa had written, donating the necklace to the Victory. Any similar donations were more than welcome. He found the outpouring of love for this hotel touching and overwhelming.

"Well, I felt pretty overwhelmed, all right. True, Saturday is still a ways off, but Mama and I are leaving tomorrow morning early for Sandusky to visit Great-aunt Clara and her family. We will not be coming back until the Saturday-morning ferry. When am I going to get back the necklace without letting our parents know what a foolhardy thing we have done?

"I could tell Joe where it is, of course, except that he and his father are in Port Clinton for a couple of days buying supplies. A note might not reach him safely. I could even run out tonight and retrieve it, but it is pouring rain, and I would not be able to see my hand in front of my face, let alone find the right spot.

"What am I to do?"

Sharing Sophie's despair, Terri flipped a page and read the next day's entry.

"Well, dearest Diary, here I am at Great-aunt Clara's house. The ferry trip to Sandusky was rather rough. I am not certain if I was seasick or not, since I was so sick otherwise. But I am better now. An idea has come to me. It may work—it has to.

"The problem is that it involves trusting someone else with a secret, and that is always dangerous. Cousin Daisy would probably be the best choice, but she is about as flighty as anyone without wings can be. Still, I could tell her that I have to sneak back to the island for an assignation with a handsome beau. That is just the sort of thing she can understand, and she will probably be thrilled to be given a secret. I doubt that she would believe the truth anyway.

"Tomorrow while Mama visits with Great-aunt Clara and a bevy of other ladies, Daisy and I had planned to spend the whole day in town shopping and lunching at a fancy restaurant. The timing will be tight, but I should be able to catch a ferry to South Bass, retrieve the necklace, replace it in Mama's room, and still get a ferry back here while Daisy is in town supposedly with me.

"She is lending me some of her old mourning clothes with a veil, the stuff she wore when her grandfather died, so no one should recognize me. Still, I will have to do a lot of sneaking. If this were not all so important, I would be giddy with excitement. Daisy certainly is, and she hardly knows the half of it.

"Now all I can do is wait and worry, and hope that

this nasty windy weather clears up by tomorrow. That ferry trip is trying, even when the water is like glass, and now as I look out the window, it seems more like a mirror broken into a thousand pieces.

"Beyond it, though, I can make out the gray blur of South Bass Island, my dear, dear summer home. Really, this game has become far more of an adventure than I ever counted on, but now the prize is far greater, too. If by playing this round, I can help save the Victory, then it will be worth all the new worry and danger. And I am sure Joe will forgive me for ending his round before even giving him the clues. After all, without the Victory, his life would feel just as empty as mine.

"Wish me luck, dearest Diary."

Hurriedly, Terri turned the page. The covers muffled her gasp. The rest of the pages were blank.

When morning finally came, the troubling thing by the window had vanished. But Terri hardly cared about it anymore. She'd spent most of the remaining night washed by waves of emptiness, disappointment, and fear. After a time, she had fallen into a fitful sleep, but it had done little to rest or calm her.

She dressed distractedly and came downstairs, earlier than usual, to find her parents just sitting down to breakfast.

"Well, to what do we owe this honor?" her mother said, laying out another cereal bowl.

"Oh, I couldn't sleep in. I kept thinking about some stuff at the excavations." Suddenly she could no longer hold back the flooding need to know. "Dad, can I ask you something about Joe Graff?"

"About Great-uncle Joe? Well, I suppose; but remember, I never knew the guy. He died way before I was born."

"Right, but did he ever get married or have a girlfriend or anything?"

Her father took off his glasses and polished them thoughtfully on a napkin. "Married? No, I don't think so. He supposedly died a very eligible bachelor. But now that I think about it, it does seem to me that there was some romantic story about that. Supposedly he did have some girlfriend, one of the rich summer people, I think. But she drowned or something, and he never got over it. Just moped around for years like he was waiting for her to come back, and then he died trying to put out the hotel fire."

Terri's mother unscrewed a jar of raspberry jam. "My, a story right out of a romance novel—and in the family too."

"Absolutely," her husband said, liberally buttering a slice of toast. "Next they'll be making a TV series: 'The Graff Family Saga'—smoldering passions on South Bass Island."

The bantering bounced on around her, but Terri just sat poking at the oat circles floating in her bowl of milk. Sophie had drowned the next day—a ferry accident to or from South Bass Island. That was why the other pages were blank. For hours Terri had been trying to tell herself that Sophie had simply misplaced her diary and had gone on recording her life in some other book. But there had been no life to record. The diary had somehow gotten left at Great-aunt Clara's and years later had found its way to an antique shop. A story cut off near its beginning. "The End" indelibly marked by a handful of blank pages.

Terri felt like she'd lost a close friend, and she'd never met Sophie. But Joe Graff had. She chewed her cereal without tasting it and admitted one more thing to herself. The Watching Boy. She knew now who he was and who he was watching for. He may have gone on living for another ten or eleven years, but in some ways Joe, too, had died the day Sophie's diary ended. The fire—the death of the Victory—had only finished things.

Terri was still brooding when her parents drove into town to prepare the shop for the day's wave of tourists. The pieces were falling together, forming an old, sad picture. But a lot of pieces were still missing.

What, for example, had happened to the necklace? Clearly it had never actually been turned over to Mr. McCreary, because the following year the hotel had closed for lack of money—partially reopening a few years later, but only as a ghost of its former glorious self. Just a handful of guests had been staying there when it finally burned in 1919.

Why hadn't the Cornwells given the necklace as they had publicly pledged to do? They had even signed donation papers. Were they too distraught over their daughter's death? Or was it not there to give? Had Sophie died on the ferry trip *to* or *from* the island?

Slowly Terri had been getting ready for work, and now she found herself standing beside her bicycle. But still the questions weighed on her. If Sophie had never made it to the island, then the necklace might still be here, hidden somewhere. The list of clues had probably stayed with the diary, and Joe had never received it.

Pulling the diary from her pocket, Terri began flipping through the back pages again, then stopped. Vividly she recalled that boy Brian slipping something out of the diary before handing it to her. An old letter from his great-aunt, he had said.

For a moment Terri bubbled with anger. But really, what difference did it make? The hiding place was probably long gone, maybe burned up with the hotel. And after all, Kelso and Stephenson did have a photocopy, so if the clues had been with the diary, they'd have those as well. Funny, though, that they'd never mentioned it. That could have brought a lot of publicity and probably money to their project. DREAMERS SEEK TO RESTORE HOTEL AND FABULOUS LOST TREASURE.

With a start she looked at her watch and jammed the book back into a pocket. Speaking of dreamers. Now she'd be late again. Hopping onto the bike, she pedaled up the drive, not wanting to look back. There just might be a figure watching out the window.

The thought filled her with more guilt than fear, but what could she do? She'd turn in the diary this morning, and all that would be over as far as she was concerned. Maybe it could never be over for the Watching Boy, for Joe Graff, but what could she do about that,

51

short of calling in an exorcist? After all, he didn't do any harm. Just watching and waiting for someone who would never come, for a game that could never end. Still, Terri wished he'd do it somewhere else.

Terri arrived at the dig clearly very late, and Mr. Stephenson just as clearly noticed. "Miss Graff," he said frostily, "if you cannot be more punctual, perhaps you had better look for a less important summer job."

She tried to hide her flash of anger. "No thank you, Mr. Stephenson. I think you'll find I have a good enough excuse this morning. I found your old diary."

His narrowed eyes widened. "The Cornwell diary? Where? When?"

Terri had been planning to tell the truth, but, frankly, she liked Mr. Stephenson even less than Brian Cornwell. The boy, after all, had been correct. It *was* a family diary, so he'd had as much right to read it as anyone—no matter what he may have filched out of it.

"That's sort of why I'm late. I was talking with a camper who said he'd found this old book near the fence. He figured it belonged to us."

As Terri reached into her pocket, Stephenson eagerly stretched out his hand. "This happened this morning?"

"He found it yesterday."

"Had he read it before giving it to you?"

Terri shrugged. "I think he just skimmed it to see what it was about."

"Hmm. Have *you* read it?"

The cross-examination made her so angry, Terri

scarcely blushed at the half-truths. "Then I really would have been late, wouldn't I?"

"Well, give it here."

Reluctantly, Terri handed him the book. Stephenson examined it, then flipped through the empty pages at the back.

"There's something missing," he declared.

"Oh? What?"

"Just some old papers. None of your affair."

"Well, all I know is that the kid said he found the book lying open with the pages blowing in the wind. If people leave important papers around outside, they should expect to lose some."

This, she realized, had been pretty cheeky, but a quick glance at Stephenson showed more suspicion than anger. He thought *she* had taken his missing papers. Why were they so important, unless . . .?

"So, it's been found," Dr. Kelso said, walking up. "Good work, Terri. Now, Keith, maybe you'll let me read the original. You've got to admit, the copy doesn't have much historic flavor."

Abruptly Stephenson thrust the book into a pocket. "But believe me, the copy is much easier to read. Faded handwriting on yellowed paper really leads to eye-strain. Isn't that so, Miss Graff?"

"I wouldn't know," she said, signing in on the time sheet.

At her dig square Terri worked diligently with her small metal trowel, but her thoughts were elsewhere. So, Kelso hadn't read the original diary, and Stephenson wouldn't let him. Why? Maybe Kelso's copy purposely didn't include all the pages, the ones on the treasure game, for example. Or the mysterious missing papers from the back of the book.

Suddenly Terri was very glad she hadn't told Stephenson about Brian Cornwell. That boy might be an arrogant tourist jerk. But, she hated to admit, he might also be something else. He might be the only person she could talk with about all this.

8

It was a productive day at work. From the number of jars and bottles they were finding, it looked as if they'd come upon the hotel pantry. But it was not a pleasant day for Terri. Every time she looked up, it seemed that Stephenson was watching her with a questioning, hostile gaze.

After work she wasted no time bicycling to Brian Cornwell's campsite, but was dismayed to see neither him nor his family's car. At least their tents and stuff were still there, so they hadn't folded up and gone home.

Too nervous to sit down and wait, she wandered around the campsite, ducking under the laundry line spread between trees and stopping to admire their tents. The big one had a label on it from one of the expensive outfitters in Cleveland. It looked as if this part of the Cornwell family was from Cleveland, like Sophie's had been, and were fairly well off too.

Brian had called Sophie his great-aunt. Then that

probably meant that his grandfather was her brother, baby Clarence. Terri smiled at the thought of the little toddler that Sophie had described in his frilly white outfits becoming somebody's grandfather. Terri looked around. Mrs. Twite, the baby's nurse, had wheeled him in his wicker baby carriage up and down the paths that had once crisscrossed this very hillside.

It was hard to imagine now, with all the wild trees and tents and picnic tables, but it had once been elegantly landscaped here. The old photos had shown well-planned paths, flowers and hedges, interspersed with rustic bridges and romantic little stone kiosks and grottoes.

Sophie Cornwell had strolled here, probably in those lacy white dresses young girls wore in those days. And sometimes she had strolled with Joe Graff. Maybe they'd stood right here on this bluff, watching the white gulls bob on the lake or the white sails farther offshore. Maybe—

"Excuse me," a woman's voice said behind her. "Are you looking for something?"

Terri spun around and blushed brick red. Here she was standing right in the middle of their camp like a burglar caught in somebody's living room. She looked beyond her questioner to see a car pulled in at the Cornwell's space and Brian coming down the path toward them, a frozen expression on his face.

"Er, yes. I'm sorry to intrude. I was just waiting for Brian. I . . . I have something I need to talk with him about."

Mrs. Cornwell smiled, and Terri knew and hated that

56

smile. It was the same one her own mother used when she thought Terri was showing some interest in a member of the opposite sex. A smug, I-told-you-so, isn't-that-sweet smile.

Terri turned to Brian and felt a confusing surge of sympathy for the kid plus a determination not to show the slightest interest in him. Neither feeling gave her any idea what to say to him, however.

He saved her the trouble. "Well, Miss Graff, I thought you might come back. I bet you want to talk about that book you borrowed."

Terri gulped. "Yes, I do. It was . . . fascinating."

"Why don't you kids go down to the beach," Mrs. Cornwell said, beaming, "while I put the groceries away and start dinner."

Brian nodded and led Terri to the weedy gulch that cut down to the beach. He growled over his shoulder, "As soon as Dad comes back tonight, she's going to gush to him about how I've met this nice local girl."

"Well, I'm not nice. I'm curious."

"About a certain paper missing from the book you borrowed?"

"I didn't borrow it. It was stolen, and I returned it."

"After reading it?"

She was silent a minute, kicking the clattering pebbles at her feet. "Yes."

Brian turned and looked at her, the breeze off the lake ruffling his hair like sun-dried grass. "So what are you going to do now?" His look was challenging.

Confused, she stared out at the white-flecked water. "Do you know what happened . . . afterward?"

He sighed. "No. I wish I'd listened better to family stories. I just know that my grandpa's big sister drowned in an accident here one summer. She got swept off a ferry in a storm."

Terri was silent a moment. "That was all?"

"No. There was some talk about a theft, too. Something valuable had been stolen from them at the hotel. I guess that, along with the tragedy of losing their daughter, pretty well soured them on the place, and they never came back."

"But that's awful! It hadn't been stolen! They pledged that necklace to the hotel, and then because they wrongly thought it had been stolen, they walked out on the place and let it sink. It closed the next year, you know."

"No, I didn't. What a mess. Here Sophie and Joe really loved that hotel, but it was their game that helped destroy it."

Feeling like she'd been punched, Terri sat down on a large rock that once had fallen from the cliff. "That's so sad. I can see why ghosts would mope around over that."

"Ghosts?" Brian's voice was sharp.

Blushing, Terri muttered, "I mean, it's like in a story."

"Oh. Yeah. I . . . was with my mother in town today, and we dropped into that little museum. That hotel must have been quite something. There were lots of pictures of the place—the fancy front, and the walks, and women walking around . . . in long white dresses."

Terri nodded absently. "It must have been awful for Joe afterward. He knew the necklace hadn't been stolen, but he probably didn't know where Sophie had kept the clues, and if he'd told the truth, it only would have made things worse. People would have said and thought awful things about Sophie and him. If he'd had the clues, at least he could have tried to get the necklace back."

"But we do have the clues now," Brian said evenly.

"You do. And so, I bet, does Mr. Stephenson."

"Mr. Stephenson?"

"He's one of the two guys running this excavation project. But . . . I don't think he's let his partner, Dr. Kelso, in on the necklace part. In fact, Stephenson was the one who found that diary in a Sandusky antique shop." She gazed thoughtfully for a moment at a gray pelican skimming over the water. "I wonder if maybe reading the parts about the hidden necklace wasn't why he got involved in this project in the first place. Maybe he doesn't care a fig about restoring the hotel but figured it'd be a good cover for tracking down the diamonds and emeralds. But if he had the clues, why hasn't he done that already and split?"

"Well," Brian said, "maybe he finds the clues as confusing as I do. He's not a native here, after all."

Terri frowned thoughtfully. "No, but I am. Maybe that's why Stephenson kept looking at me so suspiciously today. He probably thinks I have the clues and will figure them out where he can't."

Brian cleared his throat awkwardly, pride fighting

59

with something stronger. "Would you . . . would you like to try?"

She looked at him skeptically. "You mean you're thinking of tracking down the treasure yourself and living off emeralds and diamonds all your life?"

With a spurt of anger Brian grabbed up a handful of pebbles and began hurling them one by one into the water. "The thought had occurred to me. It was the Cornwell necklace, after all. But for crying out loud, how could I? Sophie's mother had already publicly given the necklace away—even signed papers, though those are probably long gone now. And, well . . . frankly, that unfinished diary is kind of hard to take. I've been thinking a lot about it, not getting much sleep. So much was left unfinished. Maybe, at least, their game could be."

Terri felt battered by conflicting thoughts. She didn't know Brian very well. Only a day ago she'd thought him an arrogant jerk. Had he really been affected by the diary the way she had? But why not? Sophie was a Cornwell, after all, and it was *his* family history she'd been writing. Sophie had been the one who'd thought up that treasure hunt in the first place.

Excitement tingled through her. Hidden diamonds and emeralds. The treasure of Catherine the Great. Sophie'd had such a talent for the dramatic. If only she had . . .

The thought of Sophie's death hit Terri like a fresh loss. It *was* wrong to leave so much unfinished. She looked away from the waves, back to Brian. "All right. Maybe we can try it. After all, we wouldn't be keeping

Stephenson from trying, too. He's bound to have a copy of the clues."

"True," Brian said, pulling a yellowed envelope from a pocket. "It would just be adding another twist to the game that Sophie and Joe didn't think of."

"What's that?"

"A race."

9

Terri threw Brian a grudging smile. No, she decided, the guy was not such a jerk after all. "Right. Let's look at the clues."

Carefully Brian slipped a piece of paper from the envelope, unfolded it, and smoothed it out on one of the tilted slabs of concrete. Together he and Terri crouched down to study the sheet. Around two edges were different-shaped medallions, six of them, holding little scenes of South Bass Island.

"It's an old piece of Victory Hotel stationery," Terri noticed. "Neat. And this is Sophie's handwriting again. Looks like a whole bunch of little poems. This first one's indented and set off with stars.

★　★　★　★　★　★　★　★　★　★　★　★　★

    " 'As in days of old, when pirates bold
    buried diamonds and emeralds and lots of gold,
    so may you, seeking treasure too,
    find a letter for every clue.'

★　★　★　★　★　★　★　★　★　★　★　★　★

"Hmm, so what do you think?" she asked Brian. "Are the poems clues to letters that together spell out where the treasure is?"

"Yeah, but not directly. I think they're clues to places where you go to find the letters. Then once you piece together the name of the place, you use the last poem—it's set off from the rest—to find exactly where to look. The problem is, if you don't know much about South Bass Island, this is mostly gibberish."

Terri spent several minutes carefully reading the poems on both sides of the sheet. Frowns rippled over her face in waves.

1. This is the edifice money built;
   it says so on the facade.
   Time sweeps away and makes all decay,
   though this letter is closest to God.

2. O, what fun. O, what a ball,
   fourth that the witch hung on her wall.

3. Norman castle of the shingle
   helps us hold together.
   Sunset arches with stone mingle,
   sinister in all weather.

4. Praise you now the laurel winner,
   raise a pillar high.
   Little ones then crowd around it;
   choose Pleiades from the sky.
   When you've found it, look around it;
   the low leopard you should try.

5. Mr. Green blinks at you, and you to him all night.
   Pulley doors on all floors, but we prefer the height.

6. Bacchus buried his true treasure deep,
   in three little rooms his jewels to keep.
   Eye to eye and loose as a tooth,
   take the first choice if you seek the truth.

7. The fairy tower that you see
   is like a grandpapa to me.
   Closer to home, alone stand I.
   My guests are visitors from the sky.

8. The lords and ladies sup together,
   and all the court beside.
   Rise to join the eastern minstrels,
   but at pinecone turn aside.

9. Small fry stutter all over their face.
   What you want is first and also third place.

10. Naiads splashing, naiads resting.
    Choose the latter for your questing.

★　★　★　★　★　★　★　★　★　★　★　★　★

In Minotaur's lair, choose with care,
second turning from the stair.
Hang your star, 'tis twelve paces far,
where elephants guard the jewels of a czar.

★　★　★　★　★　★　★　★　★　★　★　★　★

Finally Terri sat back. "This is going to be tough. Sophie may not have been a great poet, but she sure made tricky clues."

64

"Well, don't you have any ideas at all? Even I've got some half-baked ones."

She shot him a dirty look. "Sure, a few poems suggest something. Like number six here. Bacchus was the old Roman god of wine, so she's probably talking about one of the island's wineries. But a lot of winery buildings could have been torn down since 1908."

Brian scowled at the paper. "But here it talks about Bacchus burying 'his true treasure deep.' Couldn't that mean wine cellars? Those might not change much."

"True, but ... Wait a minute. Jewels. His true treasure. That's it—the Crystal Cave!" Her triumphant shout brought only blank bafflement from Brian.

She lowered her voice excitedly. "The only winery still active on this island does a business in more than wine. It's got a major tourist attraction, the Crystal Cave, right under its winery buildings. It's supposed to be the biggest geode in the world, and its walls and ceilings are completely covered with these incredible crystals. It's like being inside a jewel box."

Brian was catching some of her excitement. "And does it have 'three little rooms'?"

"Yeah, you might say so. Three alcoves, anyway."

"So when can we go? Tomorrow?"

Terri half smiled, half grimaced. They were into it now. But no one likes an unfinished game. "Sure. It's Saturday and I'm off work. You have a bike?"

"Not here."

"Then I'll meet you tomorrow morning at the rental place down by the dock. Ten o'clock."

Brian nodded and started folding up the paper.

"Wait," Terri said, pulling a slightly bent and sweat-rumpled notebook from her back pocket then rummaging for a pencil in her belt pack. "Let me copy down those clues so I can be mulling them over tonight. Some of them are probably pretty obvious if we just make the right connections."

After Terri finished her copy, Brian let her walk back to her bike on her own. Having his parents see him escorting her would just add more fuel to their misunderstanding. The girl was good-enough looking, all right, but he'd rather not explain that their mutual attraction was really to a long-dead mystery. That was something he'd keep to himself, his private shield against two weeks of boredom. Parents would either make fun or call the police—either way ruining everything.

Carefully he slipped the sheet of clues back into the envelope. Behind him the sun was setting amid cloudy streamers of orange and scarlet, casting a fiery glow over the beach. For a startled moment, Brian thought he saw another shadow stretching beside his. Then it was gone, like a sea gull in a half-seen flash of wings. White wings.

Abruptly he scrambled back up the cliff, along the gully that had held the paved walkway where gentlemen in stiff collars and ladies in white frocks had once taken their evening promenades.

Fiercely he yanked his mind away from them. This was his game now. The ladies in white had left long ago.

10

The morning overcast was thinning like the skin of a stretched gray balloon. As Brian stood by the rental shop, the sun was beginning to show through, making him less regretful over his choice of shorts and T-shirt for the day.

He was feeling a lot less confident about the day's promised activities. It sure was different from the vacation exploits his friends usually bragged about. Maybe he could get a snapshot taken of him with Terri Graff so that he could at least show them that. The harebrained scheme they were actually launching into would probably be best left unmentioned.

Finally Terri pedaled up. Her shorts and tank top confirmed that a snapshot would be a great idea, but she got right down to business.

"Okay," she said, after briefly examining the bike he'd chosen to rent, "off to the winery. But we've got to time it right. We need to be at the head of the line for the cave tour so that one of us—probably me since I'm shorter—can duck into the first little chamber while the rest are crowding around the guide in the big one."

After more instructions, Terri was soon leading the way up a steep hill, then past a cemetery, houses, and the acres of gnarled grapevines of one of the island's remaining vineyards. Finally they pulled into the winery parking lot, which was already crowded with cars, golf carts, and a gaudy excursion "train." Heading toward the imitation-German building, they at last reached the ticket counter.

"We'll skip the winery tour," Terri said firmly to the ticket seller, "and just see the cave." Opening her belt pack, she plunked down her money and looked meaningfully at Brian until he hurriedly added his. Then picking up their tickets and plastic tokens for free glasses of grape juice, she steered them into the gift shop. There they could look through a window at the crowded lobby.

Brian was just examining a key chain with an impressive amethyst crystal, when Terri jabbed him in the ribs. "Look, the line for the cave tour is moving. As soon as they're down, we streak over and become the head of the new line."

They did so and were soon joined by others. Right behind them a fidgety little boy alternated between complaining he was bored and teasing his little sister until she cried, and the exasperated parents threatened to leave him down in the cave. Finally a jabbering group of tourists climbed up from the dark hole and trooped into the lobby while a young man with a forced smile joined the new group, welcomed them to the Crystal Cave, and warned them about the steep steps.

Suddenly Terri wished she was not at the head of the line, but it was too late. The guide recognized her.

"Hi, Terri," he said, grinning at her and her companion. "I thought you'd have had more than enough of caves by now. Didn't you used to guide here?"

Terri forced a smile. "No, Jesse, that was at Perry's Cave. I'm just taking my friend here around to see the sights."

Jesse's grin focused on Brian. "Sure have found yourself a fine native guide." Then he raised his voice. "This way, folks, and watch your step."

Terri trooped down, feeling the cold slap her blushing face. Oh, well, she thought grudgingly, let rumors start flying. Brian's not bad-looking, after all. Maybe it'll make the local competition start paying a little more attention—though at the moment attention was not what she wanted.

The concrete steps were steep and slightly damp, dropping swiftly into a well-like shaft in the rock. Within several feet the temperature seemed to drop thirty degrees. The damp coolness was refreshing after the summer heat, but she knew that in a few minutes this natural air-conditioning would come to seem downright cold.

At the bottom of the stairs, the guide started talking about the discovery of the cave and how giant geodes like this were formed. With Brian beside her, Terri inched her way to the opening of the crystal cave itself, so that when the guide got the group moving again, they were the first inside. Terri slipped into the first little alcove while Brian, trying to be as bulky as he could, screened her from the rest.

Eagerly Terri looked around at the crystals that, glistening in the spotlights, lined every inch of the cave. But today her mind was on things other than their beauty. "Eye to eye," Sophie had said, suggesting that the "loose as a tooth" crystal they were seeking was at eye level. She could only hope that Sophie had been near her height.

Feeling guilty about touching the crystals, which the guides warned people against, she wiped her naturally oily hands on the sides of her shorts and began tugging at every prominent crystal anywhere near eye level. They all seemed well encased in the stone. Suddenly a large one popped free in her hand. With a surge of excitement she looked over its milky, faceted sides, then peered into the stone socket. Nothing but a mush-white slime. If there had been a slip of paper stuck in there, it and its clue had long since melted away. She had just time to whisper the discouraging news and jam the crystal back into place before the guide began herding them all out of the cave.

They trudged up the stairs after the others, rising from the clammy cold as if it were a deep ocean. Terri tried to let her disappointment fall away as well.

"Well, it was only the first one," she whispered to Brian. "There are bound to be some . . ."

Her voice trailed off as she caught sight of the first person in line for the next tour. Keith Stephenson. His eyes widened in recognition. Instead of slipping out of sight, she was forced to act casual.

"Oh, you'll love this place, Mr. Stephenson," she said with a fluttery smile. "It's just like being inside a jewel."

She walked away, wanting to kick herself for mentioning jewels. Now he was bound to know they were following the same clues. Well, that made it a race for sure.

By the time they reached the bike rack, Terri was shaking. At least Brian didn't bawl her out. "So, that was the guy who found the diary. Do you suppose he just started working on this, too?"

"You'd think he'd have started earlier. But maybe he joined the excavation so he'd have time to get to know the island and figure things out. Only now he's got to get cracking since there may be some competition."

"Well, now he knows there is, and he'll be out of there in a few minutes. Let's split."

"Right. But where to?"

"Well, I've figured out one clue that's pretty obvious. The Monument."

"Oh?" she said, a bit miffed. "Which clue is that so obviously an answer to?"

He pulled out the clue sheet from his pocket. "Number four. 'Praise you now the laurel winner, raise a pillar high.' They used to give laurel wreaths to victors in battles and stuff. And that big pillar in the middle of the island was put up to mark Perry's victory in some big battle with the British. The tourist brochure said so."

Grudgingly Terri smiled. "Yeah, you're right." Now she was scanning her own sheet of clues. "Then 'little ones then crowd around it' could mean the little pillars that are all around the monument's plaza. But what's this about 'choose Pleiades from the sky'?"

Brian frowned. "The Pleiades is a constellation—a winter one—but what . . . Oh, I get it! The Pleiades are also called the Seven Sisters. My dad's a big stargazing fanatic and is always dragging us out to look at one batch or another. This could mean we're supposed to look for the seventh pillar."

"All right," Terri said, mounting her bike. "Emeralds and diamonds, here we come!"

By the time they'd biked to Put-in-Bay, through the downtown and out to the Perry Monument, it was past noon. The grand plaza, which almost filled the narrow isthmus connecting the two parts of the island, was swarming with tourists. But rising from the center and dwarfing everything was the majestic granite pillar crowned by a huge bronze urn.

Impressed despite himself, Brian gazed up at the pale pink column rising against the sharply blue sky. Then, feeling a tug at his arm, he looked down.

"There're an awful lot of little pillars here," Terri said, waving at the stone balustrades stretching around the wide plaza. "Seventh from what?"

"Hmm. Well, since Sophie lived at the hotel, she probably used this entrance. So let's count seven in both directions from here."

They did, first going right, then left. In each case, the seventh column had no loose stones or obvious cracks where a message could be stuck. "Well, I suppose there might have been carved or painted letters that have worn away by now," Terri said rather hopelessly.

"Yeah, but what about this last part: 'When you've found it, look around it; the low leopard you should try'?"

"But there's nothing around any of these columns that looks like a leopard. No statues or carvings; not even anything with spots."

"Looks like another strikeout."

Terri stood gazing at the monument. "No, wait. Sophie might not have meant these pillars at all. There's a lot of fancy stonework inside the base of the monument. Probably pillars too, and maybe there are paintings or carvings of leopards near one."

With a whoop, Brian took off across the plaza, with Terri close behind. They slowed to wait impatiently with a group of tourists crowding in through the door.

"So when the centennial of Perry's great victory neared," a bored-sounding tour guide was saying, "this monument was constructed on what had once been a low-lying swamp. Begun in 1913, the monument was completed in 1915 and opened with a grand celebration and fireworks. Now if you will just step inside, I will show you the tomb of six soldiers killed in . . ."

Shutting out the droning voice, Terri grabbed Brian's arm. "What an idiot I am! That should teach me to pay better attention to local history."

73

"What?"

"Didn't you hear? This monument wasn't started until 1913, but Sophie wrote her diary in 1908. She couldn't have hidden a clue here 'cause it was just a swamp then."

"Oh, yeah." Brian was silent a moment. "Another wild-goose chase, I guess. Let's hope the whole thing isn't." He turned and stalked back across the plaza. "Come on, let's get something to eat. I can't think on an empty stomach."

The nearest place was the Dairy Queen, and though she hated that tourist haven, Terri headed there. She was not ready to take Brian into one of the local haunts like Tony's. She'd stirred up enough unfounded gossip as it was.

After their hamburgers and fries, Brian stopped at a gift shop, pointedly remarking that they needed some "reliable local guides." Pooling their money on a couple of pamphlets, they walked their bikes through the park, past its gazebo and stone fountain, to a bench at the north end.

Terri was still stinging from her flub with the dates. "Even these guides won't be a lot of use. They talk about a bunch of recent stuff."

"Sure, but we can still—"

"Look at the book!"

"Huh?"

"Look down!" Terri folded herself over the book. Perplexed, Brian did the same, gazing at the page showing sketches of local plants. "Mr. Stephenson's car just went by."

"You sure it's his?" Brian whispered.

"No one else would have that funky green color."

"Then he doesn't know the right date either."

Terri sat up, following the retreating car. "But he will soon, so let's see if we can't crack one of these things before he does."

"Okay. How about this one about money? 'This is the edifice money built; it says so on the facade. Time sweeps away and makes all decay, though this letter is closest to God.'"

"Hmm. Facade means face or front of something, doesn't it?"

"Think so. Hey, and money and God go together on coins, the front of coins!" Fumbling in a pocket, he pulled out a jingling handful of coins. "Look: pennies, dimes, quarters. They all say 'In God We Trust' on them."

"Right! But which letter is closest to God?"

"Oh. Two, really. *N* and *W.*"

"That's no good, then. But there are other letters on the coins. Maybe it's one of them."

Brian frowned at the coins in his hand. "No, it's different on each one, and Sophie didn't say which she meant. Wrong track again."

Terri sighed. "Well, it's got to have something to do with money and facades." She looked up thoughtfully. "An edifice is a building, right? Maybe it's a bank or a . . . Holy cow!"

"What?"

"If it'd been a snake, it would've bitten us. Look at that: the Doller Building."

Brian followed her pointing finger to see an imposing gray building at the corner of two streets. Written across the middle of the building was V. DOLLER.

"Misspelled, isn't it?"

"It's not *dollar* as in money," she snapped. "The family name was Doller. Rich local people years ago. They owned lots of stuff."

Jumping up, they both ran to the edge of the park, scattering the sea gulls that had clustered hopefully around their bench, looking for handouts.

"But there's nothing about God on it," Brian pointed out, studying the building.

"So maybe closest to God means highest—closest to heaven."

"Except that all the letters are on a straight line."

Terri scowled. "If only the word was arched up, then one of the letters would be higher." She lapsed into thoughtful silence.

Brian shrugged and dropped the fistful of coins back into his pocket. "You know, this whole thing is getting to feel like a major wild-goose chase. But if we can't find anything, at least your sneaky Mr. Stephenson probably can't either. Let's just—"

"Go to the cemetery."

Startled, Brian looked at his companion. Her face was lit with a smug smile. "There *is* an edifice where *Doller* is written in an arch with some letters higher than others. The Doller mausoleum in the cemetery, the one right near the old hotel."

Brian tried not to let himself get excited again.

"Well, at least that's on the way back to the camp-ground."

By the time they reached the cemetery, Brian was hot and sweaty and a little less excited by the idea of dia-monds and emeralds. He was definitely *not* excited by the idea of going into a cemetery—not with all the creepiness he'd already gone through around here. But at least it was broad daylight.

They leaned their bikes against the cemetery gate and walked inside. Brian had to admit that in the golden afternoon light, everything looked very peace-ful. He'd started reading the names on some of the headstones, when Terri's triumphant cry brought him trotting to where she stood in front of a small stone building. Under the eaves were carved stone oak leaves, and beneath these the date 1905. Arching over the heavy wooden doors was the carved name DOLLER.

"Well, that's it," she said proudly. "The letter closest to God is definitely *L*."

"Looks like it," Brian admitted. "And this clue is number one, so we're looking for a ten-letter word be-ginning with *L*. No sweat. Lithuania or Lindberger or something."

"Humph. Well, it's a start. If we can just fill in a few more, maybe we can make up for the ones that are missing. Come on, let's look at what we've got again."

Sitting on a grassy slope, Terri pulled out her note-book and studied the page of clues. Joining her, Brian noticed how the sun shining through the stained glass on the far side of the mausoleum burst through the

77

closest window in a glory of gold and green. He wondered whether it would really be better to be buried in someplace grand like that or just put under the grass to gradually rot back into the earth. Of course, Great-aunt Sophie had done neither. Her bones were mingled with the stones and mud at the bottom of Lake Erie. He shivered despite the sunlight, and quickly turned his attention back to Terri.

She had written an *L* beside clue number one and was making a zero beside number six. "Eight more to go. Now what about the last one. Are naiads Greek water nymphs or tree nymphs? I can never remember the difference between naiads and dryads."

"Then you had better not try," a voice said behind them. Turning with a start, they blinked at the dark figure blocking the sunlight.

"Mr. Stephenson!" Terri stammered.

11

"In fact," Mr. Stephenson continued as Terri slapped her notebook closed, "it would be better if you stopped trying a lot of things—like messing with matters that are none of your concern."

Terri's sudden pallor slid into an angry blush. "I am a native of this island, Mr. Stephenson. And matters having to do with it are a lot more my concern than they are yours."

Brian noted Stephenson's thin face and was surprised to find that the term *looking daggers* was not as impossible as it had always sounded. Clearing his throat, he stood up.

"Hey, Terri's only concern here is showing me around interesting places on the island. I don't see why that should bother anyone."

Hurriedly Terri stood up to join him. "Right. We've just been playing tourist. Nothing wrong with that, is there?"

Stephenson watched with a thin, humorless smile as

the two walked quickly to the gate. "Nothing at all, as long as that's the only thing you're playing. But some games are a little more dangerous and are best dropped. After all, as some of your recent reading might suggest, being young is no protection against games ending badly."

Once on their bikes, they pedaled furiously down the hill to the campground and didn't stop until they skidded into Brian's campsite. He was a little disappointed to see that the car was gone and remembered that today his mother had been talked into going fishing, too. He felt slightly in need of a comforting hug.

"Don't know about you," Terri said while he clamped the lock on his bike, "but that last sounded like a threat to me."

Brian nodded. "Yep. And I feel effectively threatened."

"Enough to quit this?"

He stood for a moment, staring out at the sheet of water glinting through the trees. "No," he answered at last. "Somebody's got to finish this game. And we sure shouldn't let it be that turkey."

With a squeak Terri hugged him, then, blushing, they both stepped back. Not quite the hug he'd been thinking of, Brian thought. A lot nicer, in fact.

Terri busied herself with her notebook. "Well, at least we know we're on the right track, or Stephenson wouldn't be breathing down our necks. I wonder if he thought of the cemetery on his own or just saw our bikes on his way back to the dig."

"In any case," Brian pointed out, "he couldn't have

missed the *L*. He knows as much as we do, and maybe more."

"Yeah, and he may think we have the clue from the Crystal Cave since we got there first."

"Then we'd better get to really finding some that he hasn't. Let's go over the clues, one by one. I've got these guidebooks. Maybe something will click."

"Okay, let's . . . No, I forgot—I promised my mom I'd finish painting the bathroom today, and the day's almost gone. But look, let's both put our minds to it and come up with something by tomorrow morning. I could meet you here early. It's Sunday, so I'm off again."

When his parents got back late that afternoon, they plied Brian with questions about that "nice local girl" he'd spent the day with. He didn't bristle as much as he'd have expected. Let them think what they liked. Besides, he had to admit, Terri was interesting. Not many girls he knew would get themselves (or him) involved in a situation like this.

But he was determined he wouldn't sit back and let her solve all the puzzle. The ideas he'd come up with so far had fizzled out—the coins and the Perry Monument. But there were lots more clues to go.

After helping with the hated fish cleaning, Brian settled into a tangle of tree roots at the cliff's edge and began poring over the guidebooks. After a while a pair of sea gulls fighting noisily over a dead fish drew his attention to the beach. With an effort, he yanked it back to the guidebook, turned a page, and there it was. The real answer to clue number four, as if it were outlined in neon: the Victory statue.

How dumb of them not to have guessed! The Victory Hotel had, after all, been named after Perry's victory. To honor it, they'd put up a statue on the grounds showing Victory, a lady with wings, standing on a pillar holding a laurel wreath and a staff. And the guide said it was put there in 1907. Perfect.

Excitedly, he studied the photograph. The pillar was sort of a squished rectangle, smaller at the top. Its top and base were carved stone, but mostly it was made of smallish rocks all cemented together. And edging the plaza around it were a lot more pillars, thinner and round, but all built the same way. There were more than seven.

He squinted again at the odd central pillar. Hadn't he seen something shaped like that? Sure! With some of the overgrown hotel ruins near the back of the campground.

Brian jumped up, ready to rush off exploring, when his mother announced that dinner was ready. She got very touchy about meals being eaten when they were hot. He dutifully poked at his share of fish, his mind so busy he hardly noticed the taste.

While they ate, the sun was setting into a flame-streaked lake, and as soon as they finished, he rushed for his tent, grabbed a flashlight, and took off, yelling to his parents that he was searching for a less-smelly latrine.

At first he couldn't find the spot again in the thick undergrowth. Then he saw stonework rising from the greenery like some ancient Mayan temple. Excited, he pushed in among the bushes.

It didn't take long, however, for his excitement to fade. The statue, of course, was long gone, but so were most of the pillars. He kept looking, comparing the scant ruins to the picture in the guidebook, but he couldn't figure which of the remaining ones could have been the seventh pillar from the front.

The only course was to look them all over, hoping the seventh was still there. They were all broken off fairly low, and all stood on round stone bases resting on square ones. There were no letters carved or painted anywhere, and though some of the cobbles that made up the pillars were splotchy, none could be said to have leopard spots. The photo hadn't shown any leopard statues nearby either.

Discouraged, he sat down on the cold stone curb around the main pillar. The dusk had deepened, making the bushes and towering trees look like flat black cutouts against a gray backdrop. Around and above him, the creaking, clicking insects were working themselves into full cry.

What now? He'd found the right answer, he was sure. But it still wouldn't help in finding the necklace. He wouldn't be able to impress Terri with his cleverness. Almost worse, he thought, he was somehow letting Sophie down as well.

It all seemed so sad. The doomed hotel, the prize that could have saved it, the game that could have found the prize. All so unfinished. And now, when there might be a chance to change things, it seemed as if it was too late. Too many clues had been lost. The game could never come to its end.

His eyes misted up. Through their blurriness, he caught a flicker of white and looked up.

A young girl was standing in front of the bushes. Her lacy white dress reached nearly to her ankles, and her curly blond hair was held back with a white bow. The smile on her face, however, was more impish than angelic. It seemed to challenge, almost taunt him.

He started to speak, but the words dried up in his throat. He could see the dark bushes right through her. Defensively, he raised his flashlight. The beam lit up the bushes, highlighting every leaf. But it cut through the girl as if she were smoke. Then, like smoke, she vanished.

12

Brian woke early the next morning. Not that he had slept much during the night. After that "whatever" had vanished, he'd wasted no time charging back to his tent. Then he'd lain there, wishing his parents would call off this vacation early, so he could spend a solid week on the couch at home, mindlessly watching TV.

Watching anything but ghost stories. Living one was enough.

True to her word, Terri arrived early, while Brian's mother was still frying the Spam for breakfast. To keep their conversation out of earshot, Brian scurried up to join her in the parking area.

"I figured out the one about the laurel winner," Terri announced. "It must mean the Victory statue here on the hotel grounds."

"Yeah," Brian replied sullenly. "I figured that out, too. And I looked over the ruins last night. But most of the pillars are gone. I couldn't find anything except . . ."

"Except what?"

"Terri, maybe we should give up this whole thing. I mean, it wasn't really our idea—not to start with. Maybe we should just leave it be."

She stared at him. "You mean you'd rather let that jerk Stephenson find the necklace?"

"No, no. Maybe you could just tell your Dr. Kelso about what you think his partner is doing and let us back out of it."

"Why the sudden change?"

"It's not sudden. It's been there all the time. It's just that . . . I guess I'm tired of being jerked around by . . . things on this island. Things that shouldn't be around anymore."

Terri looked at him for a long moment, then turned to gaze vaguely toward the lake. "Jerked around by ghosts, you mean."

Brian stared at her. "You've . . . you've seen her, too?"

"Her? No, him." Terri lowered her gaze to the pavement. "There's a boy who's been haunting our house for years. Always watching, always waiting for something. But recently it's been different, and I think . . . well, I think it might be Joe Graff. Great-uncle Joe."

"Oh." Briefly Brian met her gaze, then nervously he glanced away, scanning the woods. "I've never seen him. What I saw was a girl. Blond, longish white dress. Twice. The first time, after I sort of followed her, I found the diary. I didn't let myself admit that it was anything other than another camper in a nightgown. But last night at the Victory pillar, she was close. Pretty, with a cocky, I-dare-you sort of smile. Like a real person, except you could see right through her, and then she faded out."

Terri giggled nervously. "Yeah, they do that. Spooky, isn't it?"

"Very. I suppose they can't help that, being spooks." His laugh sounded forced; then his face clouded. "But they don't have to mess around with us. I don't like being used by people, whether the people are all there or not!"

"But they have to, don't they?"

"Have to what?"

"Use people. I mean, what else can they do? They're ghosts; they don't have bodies. They can't make anything happen in the real world unless real-live people do it."

"But why us? Why now?"

When Terri only shrugged, Brian sighed and answered himself. "It's because the diary has been found. Now someone has the chance to finish the game—and actually use the prize as it was meant to be used."

Terri nodded. "Which means that if it can still be found, we've got to find the necklace before Stephenson does. I could tell Dr. Kelso about it, I suppose, but he probably wouldn't believe accusations against his partner. Not unless I had the original diary, and I'm sure Stephenson's got that well hidden."

Brian was about to say something else when his mother called from the camp, "Breakfast's ready, Brian. There's plenty for you, too, Terri, if you want to join us."

Terri did. She'd felt too nervous to eat breakfast earlier, particularly with the Watching Boy invisibly peering at her from some corner. But now that she knew this wasn't just her problem, she felt a whole lot better.

As they walked toward the campfire, she quickly whispered, "Oh, I also figured out clue number ten, about the naiads. Those are water spirits, so it probably means the Natatorium—what they called the hotel swimming pool. The 'naiads resting' part probably means to look around one of the benches, but all the stuff on the deck is gone now, so it looks like we've hit another zero."

"Stephenson too," Brian said, smiling grimly.

Both Brian and Terri were glad for the less-distressing breakfast conversation. Brian's father had decided to forgo fishing for the day and do some tourist things. But even then, his main goal was fishing-related.

"According to the brochure, Ohio State runs a lake-studies program in some buildings north of Put-in-Bay. They give tours, and there's also a government fish hatchery with tours. You ever been on those, Terri?"

"Oh, sure. With school field trips, there's no way to miss them."

"Well, I'm really anxious to see that hatchery. It always fascinates me to see how they turn all those small fry into big friers."

As he laughed at his joke, Terri's eyes took on a sudden gleam of their own. "That's it!" she said, turning to

Brian. "Small fry are baby fish. And that hatchery's been around a long time." She whipped out her notebook and showed him the ninth clue.

Brian nodded excitedly, then looked up at his parents' puzzled faces. "It's sort of a scavenger hunt we're following, a game put on by the . . . the . . ."

"Historical Society," Terri chimed in. "Something to interest kids in history."

"Glad to see it's working," Brian's father said. "I take it you'd both like to go to the hatchery with us?"

"Yes, please," Brian said. "That way we won't have to take our bicycles." He looked meaningfully at Terri, and she nodded. Without their telltale bicycles, they'd be harder for Stephenson to track.

Once at the hatchery, however, Brian and Terri bowed out of the tours, saying they'd rather explore on their own. Quickly Terri lead them out on the dock, then turned to look back at the building.

"There," she said, pointing at the brickwork. "I thought I remembered some sort of odd patterns on the face of this thing."

Brian studied the building and at first didn't notice anything beyond general ugliness. Then he saw it. At the top, bricks were set in a pattern that could look like *V. O. V.* He smiled. 'Small fry stutter all over their face. What you want is in first and third place.'"

"So, our letter number nine is *V.*"

"All right!"

They both whipped out their clue sheets. "So," Brian said doubtfully, "now we've got '*L,* blank, blank, zero, blank, zero, blank, blank, *V*, zero.' Can't say that's very clear."

"Well, give us time."

"Yeah, but do we have time? So far the only clues we've got are ones in plain sight that Stephenson could read, too. And for all we know, he may have figured out some we haven't."

"All right. Your parents are still on that dreary tour. Let's work on some more of these. How about number seven. 'The fairy tower that you see is like a grandpapa to me. Closer to home, alone stand I. My guests are visitors from the sky.'"

"My guess would be the tower at the airport, except that it wouldn't have been around in 1908."

"Brilliant. Well, we know it's some tower that's sort of by itself, but that doesn't get us very far. Lots of buildings have towers."

"A church, maybe?"

"Maybe. But it kind of sounds like we're talking about two towers. 'The fairy tower that you see is like a grandpapa to me.' Maybe we're looking for a small version of a tower that Joe could see."

"See where?"

For a time Terri was thoughtfully silent, then her face lit with a smile. "Hey, if Joe had gotten to see these clues, it would have been your sheet, not mine."

"So? You copied the clues word for word."

"Sure, but the original's on Victory Hotel stationery with little scenes printed all around the sides."

Brian studied the yellowed paper in his hands.

"Right; here's the Natatorium and . . . Oh, right! I get it. Here's the tower on the Victory Hotel. Joe would be seeing that 'fairy tower' when he was reading the clues!" His grin slowly faded. "But if the smaller version was also on the hotel, it'd be long gone, too."

"But it probably wasn't. 'Alone stand I' sounds like it was off by itself somewhere else."

Brian had flipped open one of his guidebooks and was looking at a picture of the tower. "Well, it's pretty distinctive-looking. All we have to do is comb the island for something that looks sort of like it. Kind of a big island, though."

"So we better get started. We're at one end here, so we can just work through to the other."

Resolutely Terri marched off toward the point of land, about a block away, that marked the northern tip of the island. With a sigh, Brian checked to see that his parents' tour wasn't out yet; then he trudged after her, scanning every building that they passed. There was one garage with a cupola on top, but it was round, not square. Another house did have a squarish tower, but it looked a lot more modern than 1908. A bird feeder looked like a possibility, but on closer inspection it was plastic.

Suddenly Brian stopped, an excited tingle spreading through him. "Terri," he croaked, "come back here a minute."

When she joined him, Brian wasn't looking at rooftops, but at a lawn alongside the road. There, lined up to keep people from parking on the grass, were the lower parts of four columns.

"These have got to be from the old Victory monument. They're just like the ones I saw last night."

Terri nodded. "A lot of folks supposedly salvaged stuff from the ruins. You find bits and pieces all over the island. But which would be the seventh column?"

"No way to know now. Let's just check them all for 'low leopards.'"

At the second column Brian tried, he again felt that unbelieving tingle. Set in the cement down near the round base was a smooth yellowish cobble, its water-worn surface naturally speckled with clear black spots.

Hesitantly he splayed his fingers over it and tugged. It shifted slightly, but stayed in place. Another harder yank, and it popped free in his hand. He turned it over. On the back was a clearly painted letter *T*.

"Eureka!" Terri shouted. "We've found one—one that Stephenson hasn't."

Brian stood up, holding the stone to the sun as if it were a sparkling jewel. "Untold treasure in our grasp— or it will be as soon as we find a place with an *L*, a *T*, and a *V* in its name."

"Hmm," Terri said, gazing back toward the hatchery parking lot. "Then we'd better hurry up about it." A lime-green sedan was now parked a few cars from Brian's parents' car. "He's bound to see the *V*."

"But not the *T*," Brian said firmly, dropping the stone into the pocket of his windbreaker. "This one is ours."

13

They spent the rest of the morning with Terri showing the Cornwells all the sights of Put-in-Bay. At one point Brian's father grumbled about seeing every square inch on foot when there were all those little tourist trains bouncing past them on the streets. But the two kids staunchly insisted that the only way to get to know a place was on foot.

By the time Terri finally gave up and lead them to a glitzy pizza parlor, they had indeed walked along every street, and had not found the right tower. Twice they had caught sight of Mr. Stephenson until they were convinced he was actually following them, waiting for them to lead him to the clues.

"Not that I blame him much," Brian said, once they were back on the beach at the campground. The sky had clouded over, and a rising wind was slapping frothy waves against the shore. "He probably thinks we have the advantage, since you're a native of the place."

"So far that hasn't done a lot," Terri said with a discouraged sigh. "Maybe we should freak him out and start following him for a change. That would force him to either do his own thinking or give up."

Brian chuckled, then shook his head. "But we haven't time for psychological warfare—at least, I haven't. My vacation will be up in a week. Not that I'm all that useful, but I do sort of have a stake in this."

She looked at him. "Yes, you are too useful. But you're right about the time. Even if *we* could take all summer, Stephenson's not going to."

Brian stood up from the rocky shelf where he'd been sitting. "Then let's start pedaling around the island and look for that tower."

"I don't know," Terri said, eyeing the churning gray sky. "The weather doesn't look very good for that. Maybe you could start that tomorrow while I'm at work."

"I don't think tomorrow's on. My dad's been badgering me to go fishing with him, and I finally gave in. He's planning to head for Green Island, where the fishing's supposed to be extra good. That's Green Island out there, isn't it? The one with the . . ."

"The what?"

"Lighthouse! For crying out loud, it's been staring me in the face every night, and I never connected. 'Mr. Green blinks at you, and you to him all night.' There's a lighthouse on that island that keeps flashing all night. I can see it out my tent door, and if I scooch around I can see the South Bass light on that point answering it. Sophie could probably see the same thing from her hotel window—that is, if they had the lighthouse then."

"Sure they did! How does the rest go?" Hurriedly she pulled out her notebook and flipped through it, the wind snapping the pages like small flags. "'Pulley doors on all floors, but we prefer the height.' Why didn't I think of that?" Standing up, she rammed the notebook back into her jeans pocket. "You game for a trip to the lighthouse?"

In five minutes they were on their bikes and on their way. At first Brian's parents had objected because of the weather, but he assured them that they weren't going far, and Terri had something neat and indoors to show him. A few large raindrops did spatter onto them as they rode, but the scudding clouds didn't seem to be considering a very serious storm.

As they neared the lakeshore, Brian looked around, scanning the sky. Quickly he turned forward again. "Pretend you don't notice," he called to Terri, who was riding just ahead of him, "but I think there's a green car on the road behind us. Should we head somewhere else to throw him off the trail?"

She thought a moment, fighting the urge to turn around and see the car for herself. "He already knows our general direction, but maybe we can turn off at the ferry dock instead of going on to the lighthouse. If we go into the gift shop, maybe he'll think we're buying more guidebooks or something."

"Can we walk to the lighthouse from there?"

"Sure, once he leaves. We don't want him to see us head up that way."

Steadily they continued along the road, nodding at tourists on golf carts and making every effort not to look behind them. At last they swerved down into the parking lot at the dock, then spent a lot of time fussing over their bicycle locks. But when the green car came into sight, it drove right past the parking-lot entrance and continued up the road.

"Bummer!" Terri exclaimed. "He didn't fall for it. As soon as we started along this way, he must have put everything together and figured out the clue. Come on, let's run in the back way, and maybe we can still get in before he does."

Darting out of the parking lot, they raced up what soon became a graveled road. After several turns and dips, the scrubby trees gave way to a wide lawn, with the red brick lighthouse set on the crest. Gray sky and lake stretched beyond, while in front of the building were a station wagon and a lime-green sedan.

"I used to baby-sit for the people who were caretakers here—a couple of pretty bouncy kids. But they moved, and now there's a really crabby young guy here. I hope he's as crabby to Stephenson as he is to everyone else."

Slipping through the gate, Terri headed around the base of the knoll, then cut up toward the back of the house. As they reached the cover of the building, they heard angry voices from the other side.

"No, I am sorry. Like I said, this is a private residence. I do not give tours, and I do not encourage visitors. If you wish to formally apply to visit, please do so at the university offices in Put-in-Bay."

"But as *I* said," Mr. Stephenson's voice replied, "I am not an idle tourist. I am working with Dr. Kelso on the excavation at the old Victory Hotel site. We need to check the view from the lighthouse tower to see how it matches with some old photographs we have. You need not trouble yourself to give me a tour. I'll just go up on my own, look around, and come back down."

"Let's do just that," Terri whispered, scuttling off toward an enclosed porch at the back of the building. "I only hope this new caretaker isn't more into locking doors than the old ones were."

Brian followed with a jumble of mixed feelings. The sneaking around was exciting enough, but he found this building rather disappointing for a lighthouse. Instead of being tall, round, and gleaming white, the tower was short, square, and made of the same red brick as the house. But at least the window-sided turret at the top had a real nautical air about it.

Terri tried the handle of the white-framed door. It swung open silently. For a moment, they paused in the doorway, listening. Then, like a commando leader, Terri dashed to the left and through a small door.

Brian followed her up the steep spiral stairs. The confining walls were paneled and broken by plain square windows. He noticed little cupboard doors in the corners, but Terri passed these by.

"Are those the 'pulley doors'?" he whispered.

"Yeah; they used to have some kind of machinery inside that had to do with the light. But the modern light doesn't even use this tower. It's on top of that tall metal tower outside. When I baby-sat, the kids and I used to play up here, dropping stuff down the chutes. It's the top one we want, I think. 'Pulley doors on all floors, but we prefer the height.'"

Terri stopped just before even steeper steps climbed to the light platform, and unlatched a cupboard door. Brian peered inside, but saw nothing but gloom—no letters painted boldly on the paneling. He reached into his windbreaker and pulled out a flashlight. The battery was weak, but still nothing showed up.

"Maybe there's some loose paneling or something," he said, reaching in and tugging at everything he could feel. Some of the wood felt smooth, some rough and splintery. Then, in the furthest corner, he felt something else. Something was caught between two planks like food between teeth.

He closed his fingers around it and tugged gently. Nothing. Turning sideways, he stuck in his other hand and wedged his fingers into the crack between the two planks. He pried one plank forward until the thing that was stuck there came loose in his other hand.

The last person to touch this, he thought to himself, had been Sophie Cornwell. Now they stared down at the little square of cardboard in his hand. Its inked message was still plain. "An *N*," he whispered. "Look, it's an *N*."

Terri picked it up, holding it to the window light. "No, look. There's a little line along this side. I bet that's to show the bottom. It's a *Z*, I think."

Brian snorted. "Right. The mark of Zorro. Let's go."

As quietly as they could, they hurried back down the

stairs, then, after a moment's pause, dashed across the porch and out the door.

On the lawn outside, Mr. Stephenson stood glaring at them, a camera dangling forgotten from his wrist. "Pushy, aren't you? They don't allow tourists inside, you know."

"I'm no tourist," Terri said after shaking her surprise. "I'm a native here."

"Then it would be a real shame for you to lose your summer job, wouldn't it? All because of a dead, dry little game."

She flushed angrily. "Other people could lose their jobs if Dr. Kelso were to learn about the real diary."

Stephenson smiled coldly. "Funny thing, but have you ever noticed how adults tend to believe other adults rather than children? Of course, no one's job would be in danger if you turned over what you found just now."

Instinctively, Brian jammed the fist that was holding the clue deep into his pocket.

"Or if *you* do!" Stephenson snapped, jumping toward him. Brian flinched back, and he and Terri turned and ran.

Stephenson's long legs closed the distance as they all raced over the grass. He was cutting them off from the road.

Suddenly Terri veered to the right, seeming to plunge off the cliff. "Here! There's a trail," she called.

It hardly deserved the name *trail*, Brian thought as he careened down the faint parting of underbrush, then down a chain of crumbling rock ledges. Dirt and rock shot from under his feet, and twigs snapped in his grasping hands. From below, Terri yelled, "Hey, cut the avalanche." Then, with shaking legs, they were both standing on the rocky beach.

Stephenson looked down on them, a lone dark figure on the cliff above. "You two should be more careful. You could get killed that way. Just the sort of fatal accident that could happen to overcurious kids around here."

As he stepped back out of sight, Brian and Terri looked at each other, trying not to shudder. "I think he's a little crazy," Brian said.

"Or he just wants that necklace a whole lot. But then, so do I. And at least now we've got a couple of clues he hasn't. Let's go."

"Back up there?" Brian said doubtfully.

"No. If the caretaker hasn't run him off by now, Stephenson could still be lurking around. This way." She strode confidently down the beach.

The problem with the beach route, Brian discovered, was that it was not all beach. It was a series of shallow coves, stretches of beach cut off by rocky points. With difficulty these could be scrambled over, but then the cliff leaned directly over the lake, leaving no route but through the water itself. Wading knee deep (or waist deep when they slipped on mossy underwater stones) might have been pleasant on a warm, sunny day. But this was not. The wind had died down, so at least they weren't in danger of being battered between waves and cliff, but Brian wasn't sure how he'd explain this drenching to his parents.

When they finally staggered out onto a long stretch of beach, a sinking sun was firing the clouds with scarlet and gold. It wasn't warm enough to dry their clothes, but Brian had to admit it was breathtakingly beautiful. Streaks of fire seemed to flow over the lake and lap onto the beach, changing the gray stones into dully glowing rubies and turning the stone-and-brick ruins against the cliff into a vision from a fairy tale.

Brian recognized the ruins as the old lime kiln he had seen near the dock when he first landed on the island. But Terri was staring at it as if she'd never seen it before.

"Looks kind of like a Norman castle, doesn't it?" she said calmly.

"A little, I guess. Oh!" Pulling his sheet of clues from an inner jacket pocket, he looked quickly through them. "You mean like in 'Norman castle of the shingle helps us hold together'?"

"It was a working lime kiln back then, and they used lime as mortar. But I don't get the shingle bit. Doesn't look like it ever had shingles on it."

"Ah-ha!" Brian cried, breaking into a clumsy dance. "*Shingle*'s another word for beach. They use it on some of my mom's old folk-song records."

Terri was already running toward the ruin. "'Sunset arches with stone mingle' must be the red-brick arches set in the stone walls."

"But what about 'sinister in all weather'?" Brian said,

reading the clue sheet as he trotted along. "Doesn't look all that sinister to me."

When he caught up to Terri, she was standing and staring at the tower's base. "Looks like someone—guess who—beat us to it." A heap of unweathered brick seemed to have been recently pried from the left side of the arch.

"*Sinister* also means 'left,'" Brian said dully. "I remember now."

"So, apparently, did Stephenson. That's why he didn't stop at the dock parking lot. He'd already found this clue and had just figured out the lighthouse one."

With a discouraged sigh, Terri pulled out her notebook. The cover was wet, but only the edges of the pages were ruffled with damp. Flipping it open, she penciled in *Z* by number five and put a zero by number three.

"Not a whole lot better. '*L*, blank, zero, *T*, *Z*, zero, blank, blank, *V*, zero.' Not even one vowel."

The glow abruptly faded from the air as the swollen sun slipped into a bank of clouds along the horizon. Brian shivered from cold—and something more. He looked up. A figure was watching them from the cliff.

"Don't look now, but I think our rival is up there gloating."

Angrily, Terri glared upward. Brian watched as the color drained from her face. She looked away. "It's not Stephenson. It's them."

Brian looked again. Amid the brush and scraggly trees on the cliff top stood two shadowy figures. A boy in brown and a girl in fluttering white. His first surge of fear faded into regret.

"We're sorry," he yelled, more boldly than he felt. "But you didn't make it easy, you know. And time hasn't helped."

The figures among the trees were gone, but the word *time* seemed to echo back from the cliff.

It was running out for all of them.

14

The next few days on the excavation, Stephenson watched Terri like a prison guard. It seemed she couldn't look up without finding him glaring at her. She figured he was checking that she didn't go running off after new clues; but as long as he was watching her, he wasn't finding any either. Despite what he'd found at the lime kiln, he was probably at as much of a dead end as they were.

Brian met her after work one afternoon and whispered that he had deciphered another clue, though he didn't look too happy about it. "Number eight. 'The lords and ladies sup together, and all the court besides. Rise to join the eastern minstrels, but at pinecone turn aside.' It sounded like some medieval banquet hall. Then it occurred to me that that was also what the Victory dining room looked like in the guidebook. It even had a gallery up above like where the minstrels used to play. If you look really closely at the eastern stairs, you can see a carved pinecone on top of the stair post. The clue was probably hidden there."

"Good detective work!" Terri said, then sighed. "At least we don't have to waste any more time on that one. But we haven't got many clues left."

Brian nodded glumly. "Yeah, just two and seven. Looks pretty grim. Speaking of which," he said, looking over her shoulder, "so does Stephenson."

Terri shrugged. "At least he hasn't skipped off with the necklace yet. Here's the scheme I've been hatching. You go ahead like you planned and have dinner with your folks in town tonight, and spend all day tomorrow biking around looking for that miniature victory tower. Then after work the two of us will lead Stephenson on a wild-goose chase. Put on a real act. Convince him we've given up the game and are just interested in . . . other things."

"Gotcha," Brian said, thinking that this might be fun.

The next day, when Brian had again struck out on the tower question, they met at the dig after work and biked slowly into town, pretending not to see the green car following at a distance. They stopped at Terri's parents' shop for fudge and popcorn, then strolled along the dock, feeding popcorn to the pigeons and deciding which expensive-looking boat they'd like to win on a TV game show.

Finally Terri headed to Tony's Place. She'd decided that Brian was now enough of a friend to take him to the local hangout. They ordered root-beer floats at the ornate wooden bar, then wandered into the next room to watch a game of pool and talk with the other kids about their summer jobs. Everything was going well, until Brian committed the one sin guaranteed to set off island kids. He poked fun at their school.

"You've got to be kidding!" he exclaimed. "Last year's graduating class had only four kids in it? How can a school that small keep going?"

Ned, the boy he'd been talking to, squinted his eyes. "It's not the quantity, it's the quality. We've got good teachers because they like small classes and they can spend a lot of time with each kid. Almost all our high school grads go on to college. How many of your big city schools can say that?"

Brian shrugged. "Well, not many, I guess. But doesn't it get pretty boring here once the tourist stuff closes for the season? I mean, you don't even have a movie theater."

Sal, Ned's friend, joined in. "Oh, there's snowmobiling once the lake freezes over, and we put on theater of our own. I was Glinda the Good in *The Wizard of Oz* last year."

"That's 'cause you weren't good enough for the part of Toto," Ned gibed, and quickly jumped out of the way of Sal's swinging fist.

Terri took the chance to smooth things over. "Come on, school's school. The only real difference is that on the mainland they pray for snow to close schools, and we pray for fog because then the kids from the other islands can't fly in, so sometimes they just shut the school down."

While talking, she'd been steering Brian over to the window. A green car was parked halfway up the street. "Do you think we've wasted enough of his time?" she whispered. "Convinced him we have other things on our minds?"

"Maybe," he said, grinning. "But I wouldn't mind trying more of this tomorrow."

"Hey, that's not fair," she said, fighting a smile. "It's all right for you to give up. You're going away in a few days and leaving Sophie's ghost behind. But I've got Joe living—or whatever—in my house. I have to try to solve this thing."

Brian nodded. "I don't know if I really would be leaving Sophie behind. I imagine great-aunts can haunt you anywhere you go. Particularly troublemaking ones like her. Besides, I really would like to end this game— for them as well as for us."

"Good. Then tomorrow we'll meet and split our skulls over these last clues. Now, let's walk out of here like we've been having a terrific time together without giving a thought to treasure."

They did so, laughing and even holding hands— purely for effect, they assured each other. Still they each had trouble denying to themselves that they really had been having a terrific time.

They biked to their homes under another fiery sunset, but soon the clouds turned from flame- to bruise-colored, and a heavy rainstorm rolled in.

In her room after dinner, listening to the rain on the roof, Terri kept thinking about the Cornwells camped out there in their tents. It sure would be nice if they had a restored hotel to stay in. But from the conversations she'd overheard the last few days, it wasn't looking too good for that. It didn't sound as if they'd raised enough money to match the grant, and without that the hotel project was dead. The diamond and emerald necklace would sure be welcome about now.

Guilt hauled her back to the unsolved clues. She huddled on her bed, staring at her notebook. She was almost afraid to look up, in case she was not alone in the room. Think, she told herself, or you may never be alone here again.

"Okay," she said aloud. "Forget the tower; try clue number two. 'O, what fun. O, what a ball, fourth that the witch hung on her wall.'" She lapsed into thought. What do witches hang on their walls?

There was the Wicked Witch of the East, but Terri couldn't remember her walls very well. Besides, Sophie would never have seen that movie. What about Hansel and Gretel's witch? Gingerbread. Snow White's witch? Mirrors. Enchanted mirrors! That's it! Find some place with at least four mirrors.

Okay, "O, what fun. O, what a ball." Pretty dippy, really, like a first reader. But suppose it didn't mean *oh* like an exclamation, but *O* like something round— yeah, like a ball.

Immediately she remembered the Round House Bar on Delaware Street. Of course, that was a modern building, but there had been a round building there earlier. The Colonial Amusement Center, and that sure sounded like a place that could be decorated with mirrors. It had been beautiful, she remembered. And she also remembered the day it burned. She'd been just a little girl, but her family had gone to watch the fire, as had most of the island. She could still almost hear the flames crackling, see them dance into the smoke-clouded sky. The picture blended with her dream, with the other fire—Joe's fire.

Frightened suddenly, she looked up. He was there by the window, looking at her, moving toward her.

She jumped up, waving her arms as if to clear away smoke. "No! Go away! I can't help you. That clue's gone, too. Leave us alone. We can't help!"

Then, indeed, she was alone. Shaking, she leaned against the windowsill. Thunder had drowned her yelling, but it couldn't drive away the picture of his sad dark eyes. Even the lightning, flashing again and again, failed to do that.

Outside the pine trees were thrashing about like they were being tortured. One bent over so far that, in the next flash of lightning, Terri could see the roof of the old summerhouse, usually hidden behind the grove. She gasped.

After breathless moments, another bolt of lightning lit the scene. Yes. The summerhouse. The little turret on top of the summerhouse roof!

The clue had really meant it when it had said "Closer to home, alone stand I." Closer to Joe's home—right in his backyard, though the trees must have grown a lot since then. But every year the birds still made nests right under the roof. "My guests are visitors from the sky."

In moments, Terri had grabbed a flashlight and was out the door of her room. Her parents were watching TV downstairs in the living room. She slipped down to the hall closet, pulled on a raincoat, and tiptoed to the kitchen door. Then she was outside in the pouring rain, running around the side of the house. The sodden grass squelched under her feet, and dripping branches whipped at her as she dodged under them.

A flash of lightning and the little summerhouse stood brilliantly lit, but from where she stood, its roof and cupola were hidden. Thunder crashed down the night again, and the building was a dark, hulking shape. Terri ran to the screen door, yanked it open, and stepped in out of the storm.

It smelled musty and wet. She switched on her light and flashed it up to the ceiling, cringing in case she woke up some nesting birds. But it was probably too late in the year for that. Several nests of sticks and paper were tucked, empty and abandoned, under the eaves.

Paper? If Sophie had left another clue on a scrap of paper, it had probably long since become part of a nest. Anxiously Terri swept her light over the rafters. She didn't see any painted or carved letters either. Then a speck of something glinted in the light. Between two rafters, right at the peak, something gold was glinting. But it was out of reach.

Grabbing the edge of the white wrought-iron table, she hauled it noisily to the center of the little room. Carefully, she climbed on top. It wobbled but did not tip over. Reaching up, she could just touch the rafters and the bit of metal wedged between them. Touch, but not get a grip on it.

She felt around in her pockets for something to get it out with. Nothing. Then, unfastening her hair clip, she stuck the thin metal end into the crack. It caught hold. After several tugs, the golden thing wobbled, then came free in her hand.

A flash of lightning dimmed her flashlight to nothing. In her palm lay a thick metal wire curved in the shape of a letter *C*.

15

When Terri arrived at the campground early the next morning, the ground was still soaked and littered with fallen branches, but overhead the sky was a bright, freshly washed blue. She listened patiently to Brian's description of his night in a storm-battered tent.

"At least it was a bad night for ghosts, too," he concluded. "I didn't see a flicker of her."

"It didn't seem to discourage some ghosts," Terri replied. "But that's not my big news. It's this." She zipped open her belt pack and, plunking the gold letter *C* into his hand, she excitedly described how she'd found it. Then she pulled out her notebook.

"Now we've got '*L*, zero, zero, *T*, *Z*, zero, *C*, zero, *V*, zero.'"

"Hmm. With the other clues lost, it means this is all we're going to get. It sure doesn't look like any word I know."

"True, but suppose it's two words. I always thought that little jumping fish between one of the zeros and the *Z* was just a decoration. But suppose it's a word separator." She whipped out a pencil and began to write. "Then it would be *L*-blank-blank-*T-Z*, blank-*C*-blank-*V*-blank."

"Yeah, or . . . Hey, wait. That fish is shaped just like an apostrophe. The first word could be a possessive. Somebody's something or other. *L*-blank-blank-*T-Z*'s-*C*-blank-*V*-blank."

"That's it! *C-O-V-E*! Somebody's cove. We're close, really close!"

She scowled at her watch. "Look, I've got to go to work. We don't want to make old Stephenson suspicious. But take a map and pore over it looking for all the cove names. If you find a likely one, come by after work, but try to act cool."

As soon as she left, Brian scanned several maps for cove names, but though the island was clearly fringed with them, not many names had made the maps. His father was still puttering around camp, though, so Brian asked to borrow the special maps he used for fishing. These named coves galore. But none fitted L _ _ T Z's.

By noon he was pretty discouraged and joined his parents, who were poring over their own batch of papers at another table. "What're you doing?" he asked with little interest.

"Same thing you're doing, I guess," his father said.
"What?"
"Well, it looks like, with all those maps, you're trying to get to know the island better. So are we, but with a special end in view. What would you think of maybe

113

buying a summer cottage up here? The fishing is just great, and, frankly, I'm getting a little tired of traipsing all over the country each summer looking for the perfect fishing spot."

Brian's mother nodded enthusiastically.

"It'd be kind of nice," his father continued, "to have someplace stable and relaxing we could come back to each summer." Then he laughed, rubbing his nose. "Maybe it's just the Cornwell blood—family tradition and all—but I can see why those people liked this place and came back year after year. It's just too bad the old hotel is gone. I'd give anything to have that still here. Think of all that glitter and elegance, and our family right in the thick of it."

"What would you say to the idea, Brian?" his mother asked.

His head was whirling. Less than a week and a half ago he'd thought this island the dullest spot on earth. But now . . . "Yeah, a summer cottage might not be too bad. What have you got there—house ads?"

She nodded. "Real estate listings. The local paper comes out monthly. We've starred the house-for-sale ads that sound interesting, and we've arranged to talk to some real estate agents this afternoon."

"Here, we've got a couple of copies; take a look," his father said, shoving a smallish paper toward him. "You've been bicycling all over the island. Do any of the places we've starred sound good?"

Dropping his own hunt for the moment, Brian flipped through the paper. There were articles about a local swim meet, marriages, politics, softball games, church activities, a calendar of events, and a debate over the safety of golf carts. Intermixed were pictures of houses for sale.

Most looked pretty dull, but some had promise. One came with its own dock. Another looked interesting, but pretty run-down. He didn't look forward to a summer of hammers and saws. Then there was a place with a big veranda and romantic-looking trees drooping in front. He read the blurb. "The old Lentz place, nineteenth-century farmhouse. Four acres, with lakefront, barns, cave, and pine grove. A once-in-a-lifetime bargain." Sounds good, he thought, turning the page.

Then he slapped it back. The old *Lentz* place? It had a lakefront, so maybe there was a cove. No wait. There was a *cave.* An *A,* not an *O.* They'd only been guessing on vowels. This must be it. It had to be! He closed the paper, trying to keep from exploding with excitement.

"Find someplace interesting?" his father asked.

"Yeah, a couple. Maybe while you're in town talking to the real estate people, I'll bike out and look at them."

His parents left for Put-in-Bay shortly after lunch. Brian didn't think he could possibly wait until four o'-clock when Terri got off work. In fact, he knew he couldn't.

Getting on his bike, he pedaled up to the excavation site, past the AUTHORIZED PERSONNEL ONLY sign, and located Terri, sifting a trayful of dirt. He walked up to her, and when she stood up with a look of surprise, he put his hands on her shoulders and kissed her right on the lips.

"Come on, honey, why don't you knock off early

today," he said loudly, while waving the local newspaper around. "There's a great-sounding auction in town today. I want to see if I can get my dad some of those carved decoys the ad talks about."

"Uh . . . yeah," she stammered. "Sure. I've got some extra hours coming. Let me just sign out and we can go."

When they reached the posted sign-out sheet and were well out of earshot of the watchful Mr. Stephenson, she hissed, "Okay, honey, why the sudden passion for my company?"

"Cool enough, was I?" He grinned. "Just following orders. He'll never guess."

"Guess what?"

"I've got it! *Lentz's Cave.* An ad in this paper says the old Lentz place is for sale, and it has a *cave* on the property."

"Wow. Yeah, that could be it! Let's go. Stephenson can't follow us right away because Dr. Kelso's off-island today, and he has to stay and do the supervising. The Lentz place isn't far from here. I used to think it looked a little like something on the cover of a Southern romance novel."

The two hopped on their bikes and took off, casting occasional glances behind them but seeing no green car. Before long, after several turnings, Terri pulled to a stop where an old house with a pillared front porch stood half hidden behind drooping pine trees. The breeze in their dark branches made a mournful moaning. Sprouting from the shaggy grass was a new FOR SALE sign.

"I think old Miss Lentz died a couple of years ago," Terri said. "Her heirs must have finally decided to put the place up for sale."

"Isn't it kind of weird for people to have their own private cave?" Brian asked, hiding his bike in a clump of dark leafy branches.

"Not around here. My first real summer job was as a guide in Perry's Cave, and they told us that there were at least twenty known caves on the island. Years ago, a lot more of them used to be open to the public. It was a way for folks to make a little extra money—charge people for lanterns and let them go look around a cave on their property. In Sophie and Joe's time, Lentz's Cave was probably one of those."

"Well, where is it?"

Terri frowned. "I don't know. There's obviously no one living in the house to ask, and if we found the real estate people, they'd probably refuse to let us go into the cave. We'll just have to search for it."

Brian wasn't sure what he should be looking for— maybe a yawning hole in some mountainside. But when they found it after a half hour's search, he thought it looked more like a root cellar. At the base of a low, tree-covered hill, a wooden plank door was set at a sloping angle into the ground.

There was a heavy iron latch on the door, but no sign of a lock. It seemed, however, to be rusted shut. Brian started to use the heavy flashlight he'd brought as a hammer, but thought better of it and began hitting the bolt with a large rock until it slid clear. With much straining and creaking, they opened the heavy door.

Cold air flowed up out of the darkness like an escaping genie.

"I suppose this is where we use the last little verse," Terri said, notebook in hand. " 'In Minotaur's lair, choose with care, second turning from the stair. Hang your star, 'tis twelve paces far, where elephants guard the jewels of a czar.' "

"Well, the Minotaur's lair bit is clear enough," Brian said, handing Terri his own flashlight and keeping the heavy one of his parents'. "Wasn't that the Greek monster who lived in some underground maze?"

Terri nodded. "Yeah, the one with the bull's head. Let's go down and take the second turning at the bottom of the stairs."

The "stairs" were a rickety wooden ladder that felt damp and dangerously rotten to the touch. But they managed to scramble down without it collapsing. Shivering in the sudden cold, they flashed their lights around to push back the pressing dark. The ceiling behind them sloped quickly to the floor, but ahead, it rose some ten feet. The open space around them funneled down to a narrow cleft, clearly the only way to go.

At first, the walls hemming them in were dry and rough, but then they and the floor began taking on a slick dampness. The flashlight beams glinted on water droplets hanging from the ceiling.

Abruptly the corridor widened, and a smaller branch cut off to the left. Brian shone his light down it, but Terri gestured forward with hers. "The second turning, remember?"

"Yeah, just curious. I'm not a jaded, longtime cave explorer like some."

The second turning came up soon on the right. The ceiling sloped down to where a narrow cleft opened into darkness. Hesitantly Terri, then Brian, stepped through. To their surprise, the space opened into a large, low-ceilinged room. The ceiling itself was covered with little fingers of rocks, water droplets glistening on their ends. Here and there, larger stalactites stretched down toward the broader stalagmites rising from the uneven floor.

"Easy as pie now," Brian said dryly. "All we have to do is hang our star and walk twelve paces toward some elephants."

"Well, the star part, that's easy," Terri said, playing her light over the ceiling. "In the old days they used lanterns to explore the caves and sometimes drove hooks into the rock to hang them from. Ah, look there, where it's all black. See, there's a rusty hook."

They walked over to stand under the sooty ceiling. Brian looked around. "Okay, twelve paces in which direction?"

"Well, first let's see how far twelve paces takes us."

Brian began walking forward, placing one foot directly in front of the other. "Walking like this, I feel like one of those Egyptian paintings where everyone's sideways and flat. Okay, here's twelve."

Terri eyed his large running shoes. "Maybe we'd better subtract a pace or two. Your feet are probably a bit bigger than Sophie's."

Brian grunted, but stepped back. "Now what?"

"Just look around for something that's that far from the sooty spot and looks like an elephant, I guess. In these tourist caves, they give corny names to the rock formations based on what someone thought they vaguely looked like. Usually it takes about as much imagination to see it as to see the pictures in constellations."

They both ran their flashlight beams slowly around the rock chamber until Terri jerked hers to a halt. "Wait. Over there. Don't those two stalactites look a little like elephants? A big one and a little one? Their heads are humped up, then they flow down into long trunks."

"Yeah, I guess," Brian said doubtfully, walking that way. In their lights the formations looked glisteny wet, as if they were made of wax, but under Brian's curious fingers, the surface was rough as sandpaper.

"So what do we do now—dig?"

"I'm sure Sophie wouldn't have. This is all solid rock around here. We could look under stones, though."

Scattered on the floor nearby were several stone slabs looking as though they'd fallen from the ceiling long years ago. Some were clearly too big to lift and others too small to hide anything. Brian lifted one of the middle-sized stones to find nothing but a puddle of water.

With a grunt Terri shifted a slightly larger stone. Beneath it was a natural depression in the floor, and nestled into that lay an old metal box.

Wordlessly, they both shone their lights on it. The lid

was painted with an elegant woman holding something to her mouth. They could just make out the painted words FINE CHOCOLATES.

Terri propped her flashlight on a rock, then gingerly reached down and lifted the box, placing it gently on the stone floor. After a moment she tried lifting the lid. It was stuck.

Brian joined in, gripping the bottom while she tugged at the lid. Suddenly it popped open.

Inside lay a heap of rotting black silk. Through some of the shreds, they caught the gleam of what could only be jewels: forest-green emeralds and diamonds glinting like captured starlight.

Together they reached down and poked aside the crumbling cloth. Slowly, Terri pulled free the necklace, an incredibly beautiful tangle of jewels and delicate gold work.

"Much as I wanted to," she whispered, "I never really thought we'd find it."

"Oh, but I did," a voice said behind them. "In fact, I was counting on it."

16

Clutching the necklace to her chest, Terri turned slowly, knowing—and dreading—who she'd see.

Brian sputtered, more angry than frightened, "How did you find us? You weren't following this time; we hid our bikes, and you couldn't have had as many clues as we did."

"All true," Mr. Stephenson said calmly. "But you overdid your playacting this afternoon. I, too, had a copy of that newspaper you were waving around. The auction it mentioned wasn't until tomorrow, but the paper did have an ad for the Lentz house—with its own cave. I may have been a letter or two short of you, but I'm very good at crossword puzzles."

"Well, good for you," Terri said, recovering from the shock. "But *we* found it first, so we will be giving it to Dr. Kelso when he comes back."

"Oh, I think not," Stephenson replied, smiling thinly. "I have been looking for that necklace a good deal longer than you, I found the diary, and I have better plans for the Czarina's jewels than letting Kelso squander them on resurrecting some useless ruin."

"Sorry," Brian said firmly. "If you read that diary, you know that the Cornwells publicly gave that necklace to the hotel, and that's where it's going."

"That, I'm afraid, is ancient history. And so will you both be if you don't hand me that necklace now."

Still smiling, the man pulled a revolver from his pocket and aimed it at Terri. She gasped, then almost shrieked as she caught a flicker of something white out of the corner of her eye. Stephenson must have seen it, too. Instinctively he glanced that way. Leaping forward, Brian cracked his heavy flashlight down on Stephenson's hand.

The gun went spinning over the stone floor as Brian and Terri charged out of the little room.

They hadn't gone far down the passage when Brian, now holding their only flashlight, skidded to a halt. "No! We've gone the wrong way!"

They turned, but already Stephenson's light was in the passage behind them. Turning again, they kept running. Twice passages branched off, and randomly they ran down one, then another. Then Brian's jostling light showed a dark emptiness close to the floor. He paused a split second, then knelt down and crawled through. Terri was right behind.

Crouching under a three-foot ceiling, they scuttled to where a series of stalactites and stalagmites met in a jagged screen.

Even hunched down, Terri was afraid they would be

seen if Stephenson shone his light in there. Inching back in the dark, her foot slipped into water. She probed it. Cold, deep water.

Tugging silently on Brian's sleeve, she moved backward, lowering herself into the cold pool. In there, with only their heads sticking out behind the rocks, they'd be completely hidden. Brian eased into the icy water beside her, just as they heard Stephenson's voice in the passage outside.

"All right kids, give it up. I know you didn't make it out. You're still here somewhere." After a moment, a beam of light sliced through their little stone cell. It missed their damp hiding place.

Then the voice sounded from farther down the passage. "I can wait as long as you can, you know. But if I get fed up, I can always go off and lock the door. After a month or so, once the search is over, I can come back and pry the jewels from your dead fingers."

A long silence, then the voice came from back the other way. "I'd rather not do that, though. Give me the necklace, and you can live. I've got my escape planned, so you can blab to Kelso all you want, but I'll be safe."

Yes, Terri thought, but you'd be even safer if you took the necklace and locked us in anyway. Moving quietly in the water, she unzipped her belt pack and stuffed the necklace inside. Her hand was sore from clutching the sharp stones.

"When you decide to cooperate," the voice called again, "just come slowly up the passage toward the stairs. And no more tricks with fluttering white things."

Terri figured it was safe to whisper. "Did you flutter anything white?"

"No."

She thrust the obvious next thought aside. "There's got to be another way out of here."

"I didn't notice any," Brian said gruffly.

"Well, we could crawl out of this hole and sneak down the corridor the other way. Or we could try one of those side passages. Some caves have two entrances."

"Sh. He's probably creeping back this way now, trying to hear us."

Annoyed, she lowered her voice. "Well, then, stop thrashing around in the water. The waves slapping on the rock will give us away."

"I am not thrashing."

And it didn't really feel as though he was, Terri realized. But something was making the water around them rise and fall. Cave pools were usually deathly still. This was more like . . . the lake.

"Let me have the flashlight," she whispered, grabbing it from his hand before he could protest. She shone it down into the dark water.

"Hey, cut the light. It'll give us away."

Terri ignored that. "I think this pool is connected to the lake. If the connection's short, and wide enough . . ." After a moment she asked, "Is this light waterproof?"

"Supposed to be."

Taking a deep breath, Terri slipped beneath the icy surface. In her moving light the water glowed a soft blue-gray. Then she saw a slash of deeper blue where their shallow pool dipped downward. She bobbed her head up, took another breath, and wriggled like a fish toward the inky patch.

It was a long, low gash. Grabbing the lip of the rock, she pulled herself down. Her light swept ahead, showing a watery blue tunnel. Tight, but not too tight. She could fit. She switched off the light.

Darkness pressed in, but after a moment she could see a faint smudge of light at the far end. She stayed down until her lungs couldn't take any more, but that distant light still showed.

Letting go of the rock, she rose to the surface. "Is he near?" she whispered as water dripped down her face.

"Don't think so. Thought I heard him a second ago, but from pretty far off."

"I think there's a passage to the lake through here. I saw some daylight. I'm going to swim through there, then come back and tell you if I'm right."

"Hey, let me do that."

"Don't go all macho. It was my idea. Besides, I'm skinnier than you."

Taking several deep breaths, Terri switched on the flashlight, then dove again. Pulling herself to the stone gash, she wiggled through. The passage seemed narrower than it had and the light farther away.

Half swimming, half crawling, she moved onward, fear beginning to grow. Holding the heavy flashlight slowed her, and the rocks seemed to be trying to as well. They jutted from all sides, scraping and bruising her as she flailed past. The water itself pushed at her with surging underwater waves.

Her chest began to ache. She wasn't sure she could make it, but now it was too far to turn back. And there was no way to turn around in this narrow tunnel. The rock and the water seemed to crush in on her. Panic burned through her, searing her lungs. Was this what it felt like to drown? Was this what Sophie had felt?

Suddenly the water was a pale, glowing blue. Feebly, she squirmed free of the rock and rose upward. Her head burst into sunlight—sunlight and air. Taking gasping breaths, she hugged a slimy green rock and giggled with relief. The wide blue expanse of Lake Erie had never looked so beautiful.

It was long minutes before she could force herself back underwater, back along that horrid passage to the cave pool.

Brian was waiting for her, shivering in the dark, but whether from cold or fear, she didn't know. It ought to be fear, she decided, but didn't tell him.

Instead she whispered a description of the way out and stressed that he had to take in as much air as he could, then move as quickly as possible. He could take the light, and she would follow right after him.

Finally Brian dove down, but Terri could barely make herself follow. When she did she found it wasn't quite as bad as before. Ahead of her Brian's body blocked most of the light, but it was easier to move with both hands free. And she did have the comfort of knowing that this trip could be done.

When at last they were both breathing sunny air and hugging the moss-slicked rocks, Brian looked at Terri, his face as pale as a dead fish. "That was the worst minute in my life. And you did it three times."

With a weary smile, she nodded. Then, fighting the steadily rolling waves, she swam out farther from the cliff. "Let's look for someplace we can crawl ashore. If I stay in this water much longer, I'll freeze solid."

She swam west along the coast until it was shallow enough to walk. Soon the cliff gave way to a small, hemmed-in beach. Feeling heavy and cold as lead, they staggered out and collapsed onto the dry, sun-warmed pebbles.

Terri lay back, happy to sprawl in the sun forever.

Hazy moments passed until an unexpected voice jerked her awake. "What's this—a couple of beached fish? Must be those blind cave fish you always hear about. Figured I ought to check out all the cave passages. What good fortune one should lead to such a charming *isolated* beach."

Suddenly Terri felt too tired and miserable to even sit up, but beside her Brian was crouching like an angry cat. "Give it up, Stephenson. These jewels aren't meant for you. Can't you see that? They were meant to help the Victory, and that's where they're going. The game's over."

"Not quite," the man said evenly. "The last round is where, regrettably, two troublemaking youngsters are mysteriously shot and their bodies hidden in a cave, not to be found for a good long time."

"Not a very likely outcome," another voice broke in. "Not with so many witnesses."

Crouching now beside Brian, Terri looked way up. Someone was standing on the edge of the cliff that walled in their little beach. Dr. Kelso.

Stephenson glared at Terri and Brian, then back up at Kelso and the metal object flashing sunlight from his hand. After a frozen moment he turned and dashed back into the narrow crevasse leading to the cave.

By the time Brian and Terri stood up, Dr. Kelso was already scrambling down to the beach. He skidded the last few yards in an avalanche of dirt and stone, dropping the archaeological trowel he'd been gripping in his hand. "I wonder if Keith thought that was a gun," he chortled when he reached the children.

"Dr. Kelso," Terri blurted, "how did you find us here? I thought you were off-island."

"Hey, shouldn't we be trying to stop Stephenson?" Brian interrupted.

"The park ranger waiting at Keith's car will do that," Dr. Kelso replied. "But it really is amazing that I found you at all—and in time. I came back from the mainland today much earlier than I'd planned. I had been checking on some of Keith's financial claims because things hadn't been matching. I'd discovered that his supposed financial backing of this project is mostly fake. In fact his whole business empire looked on the verge of ruin.

"I was furious and wanted to confront him with it, so I stomped right into his trailer in the middle of the day, but he was out. Instead I found the *original* of the diary, which he'd always kept me from reading. That made me as curious as I was mad, so I started flipping through it and discovered the pages left out of my copy.

"I took them back to my trailer and read them. When I finally fit all the pieces together, I was twice as mad as before, so I barged back to his trailer. The door was open and a copy of the local paper was spread over his table with an ad circled and the word *cave* underlined. I found out from the rangers where the Lentz place was, and we drove out here."

Terri brushed the water-frizzed hair out of her face and asked, "But how did you find us down here?"

"I was tearing around this farm searching for Keith, when I saw a couple of kids standing on that cliff looking down like something really interesting was happening below. By the time I got there, the kids were gone, but I saw you two on the beach and that erstwhile colleague of mine coming out of the cave, gun in hand."

"Oh," Terri said tautly. "And those kids—was there a boy in brown and a girl wearing white?"

"That's right. Friends of yours?"

"In a way."

After a moment, Terri unbuckled her belt pack and handed it to Brian. "This really is your family's to present—at last."

Then she turned back to Dr. Kelso. "I'm sorry. I guess you two haven't been introduced. This is Brian Cornwell, Dr. Kelso."

"Cornwell?" the man said, raising an eyebrow.

Brian was looking down at the pack in his hands. There was a fortune there—a family fortune. But no, it wasn't really a Cornwell's to give or not give. That decision had been made a long time ago. Besides, with the way his dad felt about family history, Brian knew he'd approve.

Unzipping the pack, Brian pulled the sparkling handful of diamonds and emeralds into the sun. "This part of things never got finished before, sir, but the idea was to use this for the Victory Hotel. I hope it still can be."

The man looked astonished, then deeply happy. "Yes, I believe it can. This can make all the difference." He burst into a triumphant laugh. "The Victory will rise again!"

After telling Dr. Kelso their slightly altered stories, Brian and Terri followed him—by an easier path—up the cliff.

Terri looked around as they climbed. "Do you think *they'll* be around to see the new hotel built?" she whispered.

"Maybe. Or maybe they just had to stay around long enough to see that game of theirs finally come out right."

When they reached the top, Brian turned to Terri and grinned. "But *I* intend to be around to see it. After

131

all, my folks are looking for a summer house right now. And I personally know of a once-in-a-lifetime bargain with four acres, beachfront, and a cave of its own."

Grinning back, Terri grabbed his hand. "Watch out. Before you know it, you'll be almost a native of this place."

"Yeah. And loving every minute of it."

AUTHOR'S NOTE

When the Victory Hotel opened in 1892, it was hailed as one of the most elegant, modern, and fashionable resorts in America. Among its luxuries were electric lights, trolley service, and a co-ed swimming pool. The hotel's history from its glory days, through financial hardship, to its loss in the spectacular fire of 1919, is much as I have presented. Sophie Cornwell and Joe Graff, however, are my own creations, as is the diamond and emerald necklace.

If they had existed, though, their story might have played out as it did here since the settings on South Bass Island and the clue-hiding spots are all real—with the exception, of course, of the final cave which is as fictitious as its treasure.

My special thanks to the people of South Bass Island and Put-in-Bay who knowingly and unknowingly helped me put this story together. Theirs is a lovely island with an exciting romantic history. I could wish them no better gift than the one I dreamed up—that someday someone might rebuild their glorious Victory, with or without the help of a lost necklace.

Test #15827
R.L. 5.6
Points
5.0